After David

Catherine Texier

ITNA PRESS
Los Angeles, CA
www.itnapress.com

This is a work of fiction. Names, characters, places, and incidents are a product of the author's imagination. Locales and public names are sometimes used for atmospheric purposes. Any resemblance to actual people, living or dead, or to businesses, companies, events, institutions, or locales is completely coincidental.

Catherine Texier. -- 1st ed.
ISBN 979-8-9882829-1-4

Library of Congress Control Number: 2023950545

"Age doesn't protect you from the dangers of love. But love, to some extent, protects you from the dangers of age."

—Jeanne Moreau

1

LOGGING ON THE site is like stepping into a candy store. Or walking into a party and waiting for someone to talk to you, some swaggering dude with a joint in one hand and a bottle of beer in the other. Except *he* is the only one you're waiting for.

All you've got to do is leave your chat window open, and the hot pink band will light up and they'll rush in. One of the many amazing surprises of dating online in your sixties is to discover all the twenty-somethings and thirty-somethings who flock to you as the latest taboo to transgress.

Ethanb, 20 – You're really attractive. It's my fantasy to be with an older woman.

BMW1976, 37 – I love French women

Desire4Mature, 42 – The dynamic is unmatchable when it's the right older woman and a younger man.

Eljefe86, 27 – I know I am a bit young but I think you should give me a chance…

How could I resist clicking?

2

THE FIRST TIME we met was in Tompkins Square Park, around noon, before he went to his day job at a nearby recording studio. He had contacted me on the dating site a couple of weeks earlier. *Hi, I am Jonah, you seem quite lovely.* I liked that word *lovely.* Almost old school, anachronistic, even. So much more respectful and charming than the raunchy pick-up lines guys on the site tossed like so much hastily knotted bait in the dating river. A touch of old-fashioned gallantry that contrasted with the pictures of this cool guy, sexy as hell, with his scruffy beard, dark curly hair, beat-up pair of Converse, and an electric guitar on his knees.

Still, when I saw how young he was—thirty-seven—I hesitated. I was sixty-two. A full generation older. He gently insisted. I gave him my phone number and he called me. His voice was smooth, just a little nasal, relaxed. Not pushy. When you meet someone online, you make your decision to go ahead or not on tiny clues. He worked two blocks away from my place. Why not get together for coffee?

It was mid-September, a few days after my birthday. The weather was warm, with a trace of cool, the elm trees still glorious, their green just a bit dusty after the hot summer. I waited for him by the dog run and watched a pair of pit bulls frolic. I had an envelope under my arm, with my bank statements proving I could cover Louise's rent in Brooklyn in case she came short. I had to have everything photocopied so Louise could sign the lease. I was nervous about whether I had enough money in my relatively small investment account to qualify as guarantor. New York landlords require solid cash in the bank.

I was still getting royalties from the book I had written about the end of my marriage with David, but they were dwindling, so I was mainly living off my teaching and my paychecks as a freelance commercial translator. Louise and Juliet were at home, Juliet visiting from Jacksonville with Vivian, her baby, who was now exactly one year old. I didn't tell the girls I was going to meet him. I just said I was going to the copy place. I wasn't dressed for a "date." Skinny jeans, T-shirt, denim jacket, booties, casual. My usual look.

He was a jazz guitarist. No point dressing up. He strolled up to me in his sneakers and bomber jacket, looking straight out of Brooklyn. Laid back. Cool in a kind of nerdy-sexy way. Jewish, I realized later when I looked his quartet up online. Dark hair curling in his neck and tumbling forward, dark stubble of a beard, sensual mouth, soulful look in his green eyes, strong—but not too strong—nose, tallish, but slight. Elegant. Sexy smile. Where had I seen that smile before? These warm, smoldering eyes?

Shall we have coffee? he asked.

As we walked side by side across the park, falling into step with each other, he felt familiar, as though we had been lovers in a previous life. I forgot the envelope under my arm, the financial responsibilities. There was a quality of silence around him that I found relaxing, a mute complicity, as if his presence released in me a long-forgotten insouciance. He was immensely appealing.

We headed to the little coffee shop along the park. He asked me if I had told my daughters I had a date. I said I hadn't. Then he asked me if they were his age. I said, no, younger. And we laughed with relief. At least, that was that. And then his smile, head a little to the side, almost shy as he offered to pay, because I was taking out my own wallet, not sure. Was that even a date?

I told him I had to photocopy some paperwork, and he offered to walk me all the way to the copy place (*I'll be a little late for work, but that's okay*). Later, I thought he had arranged our date close to the time he had to start work, so that if we had no chemistry, he would have a good excuse to cut the date short. We got out, coffees in hand, and I spilled some on my feet. He squatted to clean up the stain with a napkin and said he liked my boots, and I handed him my cup while I went in.

While I waited for the paperwork to be photocopied, I thought of David and of our move to the neighborhood more than twenty-five years ago, when everyone lived in the Lower East Side instead of Brooklyn. Writing the first short stories, sending them out, applying for grants, selling articles, writing all day long, giving readings and going to readings every night, scrambling for money, the excitement of belonging to a group of young, edgy, emerging writers. I could sense, or guess, he was holding out for the same dreams. Did he see that in me too? Or did he only see an older, attractive, French woman with whom he wanted to experience the thrill of the forbidden?

I was surprised he was dating online. He was in a band. He must have girls fawning all over him.

He laughed.

Actually, the kind of music I play, it's all guys. It's not like pop music. I don't get to meet girls that much. And people are so guarded in New York. If you talk to a girl in the street, they think you're a creep.

Why did you contact me? I'm so much older than you.

I thought you were cute.

I hope it's not because you're into older women. I wouldn't want to be a fetish.

His face didn't give anything away. He would be a good poker player, I thought.

He had dated a German woman for three years, he said, going back and forth between Berlin and New York, when she finally moved back for good a few months ago, and he stayed in New York for his music.

I told him I had been in a relationship for six years with a Russian guy who worked for the UN in Geneva. He asked me to go and live with him. But I didn't want to uproot my life and my daughter's life. Besides, Geneva's deadly. Berlin's better.

That's when I asked him the name of his band. He was playing tonight, but way out in Bushwick (*I'm not going to ask you to go that far*). Then he pointed to a metal door covered with graffiti in a grimy block that gentrification hadn't reached yet.

I work here. It's a recording studio.

I double-kissed him, French style, and on the way back home, I sipped my cappuccino with the kind of lightness and excitement you feel after the promise of a new love or a promising encounter—such an unexpected surprise, tendrils of desire rising in a limpid sky, not a cumulus in sight, thinking no further than the moment, no further than that immediate mutual attraction, that ease we both felt, then joyfully tossed the cup in the trash can at the corner before walking up to my apartment.

He sent me a message two days later. I was in a taxi headed to JFK with Juliet and Vivian. Juliet lived in Jacksonville with her husband who was a jet pilot in the Navy, and I was going to spend a few days with them while Scott was away on a deployment.

On my way to Florida, I texted back. I glanced at the baby who was wailing while Juliet precipitously unbuttoned her top and pulled out a breast dripping with milk. The driver, who looked Afghan or Uzbek, stole a quick, possibly disapproving look in his rearview mirror but said nothing.

I only mentioned that I was traveling with my daughter. I didn't mention the baby. Her existence was off-limits, of course. Unmentionable. Unthinkable.

Let's get together when you come back, he texted.

3

IT WASN'T MY first experience with virtual encounters. One day, a couple of lonely years after my breakup with Vadik, *Irishactor* sent me a direct message on Facebook. On the thumbnail photo, a sexy guy in his thirties, with pale blue eyes, cropped hair, and a light beard, looked thoughtful. His page was filled with dreamy photos of a farmhouse by the ocean, shots of a white mare peacefully grazing in the fields, the rocky Irish coast in the background, and of a stone fireplace in front of which a Persian cat slept, its paws folded under its bosom, next to an open laptop.

We started to message every evening—which, for him, being five hours ahead on the west coast of Ireland—often meant three or four a.m. But he was a night owl. I imagined him in the rugged farmhouse, within hearing distance of the tide, waves crashing menacingly on stormy nights. And me, flying to Dublin and showing up soaked from the diluvian rains while he greeted me, bathtub full of steamy water, fragrant Irish stew (he had given me the recipe) on the stove. The affair lasted two months. I was stunned to feel how powerful the letdown was afterward, as if we'd literally spent all our nights together, flesh to flesh. I knew imagination was the most powerful organ of desire, but here was the proof of its power.

After *Irishactor*, signing up on the dating app was an easy step, like shifting from smoking weed to shooting hard drugs. I had no expectation, really, just a bit of excitement: choosing the photos, writing the profile, and the trepidation of exposing myself publicly, as though I was about to stand half-dressed in a skimpy outfit on a street corner, waiting for the first clients to show up.

Justpassingby, 42, Manhattan, PhD in literature from Brown, worked in advertising. No photo. But the picture he sent me on a bucket site was very cute, at least what I could catch of it before it got swallowed up in cyberspace. Smart and fun and a good flirt. A girlfriend who traveled a lot for her job. Did I mind? I did not.

We'd log on in the evenings and I'd take my computer to bed or chat on the app on my iPhone. What are you wearing? Usually a plaid pajama bottom and a tank top, or some evenings, just the tank top because it was May and it was getting warmer, and one thing led to another. We both watched *Mad Men* and debriefed afterward from our respective beds. Did you see Megan tonight? I don't like her. Too big a smile. Tonight it was really dark. Do you think he'll end up killing himself, throwing himself out the window? He was extra cautious. No photo and no personal details on the site, no mobile number, only instant message on the app, and he only gave me his first name. Matt.

One evening, a few weeks after our first contact, he jumped the gun.

Do you want to meet tonight?

He picked a bar in K-town, on the first floor of a hotel. The bar was deserted, with a *Lost in Translation* lounge vibe, a Korean barman wiping glasses behind the counter pretending not to pay attention. Matt was sitting at the bar, in the corner. I slipped on the stool next to him.

He was good-looking, preppy-cool, short dark hair, blue eyes. Dark jeans. Blue canvas jacket. Would I have been attracted to him if I'd met him cold here in this deserted bar? We were already way past that. We sat on a couch. After a glass of chardonnay, he leaned toward me. Shall we kiss? Thirty minutes later we were breathlessly making out in the cab taking us back to my place. I didn't invite him up.

A week later, he booked a room in a hotel in Soho and waited for me, reading a novel by Ann Patchett. *Bel Canto*. Good choice, I said. The room was lovely, elegant, all shades of taupe and gray. I was wearing a long, black summer dress I had just bought and flat sandals. He sat next to me on the bed and ran his hands up my naked legs.

The late afternoon sun filtered a soft light through the sheer curtains. No noise came from the street. A big mirror on the dresser played our reflections, streaked with splashes of slanted sun. It did feel like New York, but a foreign New York we were both visiting for the first time, coming from other, far-flung countries, and we had just met and booked a room.

We were good together. The chemistry, the fluidity of our moves. A perfect bubble out of time and place.

It was a shock, afterward, to be back in bustling Soho, warm, sunny. I floated back home, in sex afterglow.

We stayed in contact for a while. And then I didn't hear from him for a couple of weeks. One night he messaged me and apologized for being out of touch. He wasn't single anymore. I liked that he had been gracious enough to let me know. One day when I looked for him on the site, I saw he had deactivated his profile. I knew it would just be a fling since he had a girlfriend. But I was grateful for what he had given me: the reassurance that I was still desirable, still sexy, still vibrant.

4

FOUR MONTHS LATER, *Hey11211*, 37, Brooklyn, jazz guitarist, appeared in the flesh between the elm trees of Tompkins Square Park, having magically slipped off the small window of the dating app like the genie floating out of Aladdin's lamp.

Hi, I'm Jonah, he said.

Almost instantly, it felt like love.

I couldn't say why, exactly. Of course, all the red flags shot up simultaneously—wide age difference, casual online contact, jazz guitarist, laid back attitude, non-date coffee date creating a perfect storm of arousing danger, making my heart beat. But at the same time, this uncanny feeling of complicity, as though we had already slept together, and we could just seamlessly slip into bed without missing a beat or embark on a trip tonight. Last minute tickets to the Maldives, for instance.

I couldn't remember when I had the dream, whether it was after the first or second time Jonah had come to see me. But I'm pretty sure I hadn't had it in Jacksonville at Juliet's, although when I was there, I woke up several nights in a row in a sweat, wondering whether I should pursue him or not because he was so much younger. But when had I ever put the brakes on anything in my life, especially where men were concerned? All the men I had been with since David were younger than me, so what was an extra few years? Thinking back, I must have had the dream after the first time we had sex, or maybe after he'd asked me online about anal sex, the word *anal* blinking dangerously on the little window coiffed by a band of hot pink. I was being pursued by two black wolves, up the stairs of a house I shared with my mother. The wolves had cornered me against the wall. I woke up, drenched in sweat.

He texted me the afternoon I had flown back from Jacksonville. I was doing some errands in the neighborhood, and my phone buzzed. I thought maybe it was Louise. I fumbled to pull my phone out of my bag and when I saw his name, my breathing accelerated.

Hey Eve. So when are you going to invite me up to your place?

Me: *Why don't we have a drink tomorrow and talk about it?*

Him: *I think you've already made up your mind.*

I thought of that line from a song that had been a hit all summer: "*I know you want it, I know you want it.*" My heart beat a little faster. He was right. We had both made up our minds within a few seconds of seeing each other.

He continued: *Considering our age difference, it would play out like an affair rather than a romance.*

I was walking through the park, phone in hand, close to where we had first met, coming back from depositing a check at the bank (later he would show me how to deposit checks directly on my phone, and I downloaded the app). It was a sunny day, but the light seemed to darken, as though a cloud was passing in front of the sun. I shivered and sat on a bench. So that was his opening gambit. All risk and benefits calculated beforehand. I just want to fuck you. Let's not waste our time in niceties like dates and candlelight. That's the deal, take it or leave it. No room for negotiation. I swallowed hard.

Fine, I thought. He only wants sex? I can handle that.

I played it coy to hide my agitation. *What about seduction?*

Him: *Yes, seduction, of course. Always seduction.*

But my legs felt weak when I got up and started to walk back home, as if he had already backed me into a corner and taken control. I didn't know whether I was disappointed or aroused, the two sensations blending in an explosive mix.

Later it occurred to me—how could I have not realized it at the moment, how could I have been so blind—that it was no coincidence I had met Jonah just as Louise was about to move into her first apartment, and just as I was leaving behind the role of mother. That I would try to make him fill a void left by Louise's moving out, Louise who had filled the void left by David's absence.

After the breakup with David, I couldn't wait to shed the role of wife, like a snake sloughing its skin. The truth was that I was shell-shocked. I couldn't imagine embarking on a new relationship. With whom? How do you start again meshing your life so intimately with someone after a twenty-two year marriage? My body was running way ahead of my emotions. The sudden freedom was intoxicating. All I wanted was lovers. Hot sex. Right away there were a few, in quick succession, fleeting, passing by. And then there was Vadik, who was living far away in Europe and travelled all the time for his job at the UN.

The long distance didn't scare me. On the contrary, it allowed me to be a mom for Louise without confusing her by bringing a man into our home on a daily basis. In fact, when he asked me later to live with him in Geneva, I panicked. I couldn't see myself moving with Louise, being a wife in his apartment complex in the outskirts of Geneva, which frighteningly resembled the Soviet-era apartment buildings in Moscow where he had grown up.

And now, just as Louise was about to leave home, I felt a new burst of sexual energy. It was a funny, unexpected thing that in my sixties I felt more self-confident than I had been at fifty when David had left, or even at thirty when we had met. I looked younger than my age, like my mother did, slender, toned body and a halo of blond hair. Lucky genes, I guess. I also had in me that fire she had. I was jealous of her fire when I was a girl, when she lit up a room with her energy, her seduction, sucking up all the attention to herself. My own fire had just been smoldering all these years in the safety of the couple. And I believed that charm, seduction, and vitality came from an inner radiance, not, or not only, from youth.

In *La Maman et la Putain, (The Mother and the Whore),* the Jean Eustache movie, Alexandre, played by Jean-Pierre Léaud, has a live-in girlfriend, Marie, but starts an affair with a hot Polish nurse which threatens his relationship with Marie.

I had grown up with that story, the constant swing between pure wife and naughty lover, the oldest story of romance as told by men in the Western world and perhaps in the whole history of humanity. My family had embodied that split. In my grandparents' home, where I grew up, my grandmother played the wife and mother. Her role was to keep everyone fed, clothed, educated, and controlled, while my mother, defiant and pregnant by accident, was the bad girl with the platinum blond hair and the stiletto heels, cigarette dangling between her fingers, whose mysterious life played out offstage. I navigated between them, the straight-A, straight-laced good girl, secretly yearning to let my wild side loose as soon as I could.

With men, I was always torn between the two, even way back when David and I had gone down to City Hall for a shotgun wedding, one month old Juliet in her little bassinette at our feet, and even years later when Louise was born.

5

HE TEXTED ME the following Monday, midmorning. I was getting out of the shower, thinking about him.

When will you invite me over?

An hour later he was running up the stairs, his guitar case slung over his shoulder. It was noon. The sun was pouring in. I made him espresso in my stovetop Italian Moka pot. Dark and lanky, he watched me with a look of expectation and ironic detachment, perhaps not sure what I was expecting of him. And I watched him watching me. While the coffee was brewing, he strolled to the baby grand piano and opened the lid.

Better not, I said. It needs to be tuned. The wood got cracked when it was shipped from France. It was my grandparents' piano, from the thirties. I played on it for ten years.

Afterward, I regretted not having heard him play. I remembered my mother talking about a lover she had had—a Jewish concert pianist—as a "grand tenor," which I imagined alluded to his male seduction, (or, who knows, perhaps even to his lovemaking), an expression that seemed appropriate for a musician. Jonah didn't strike me as a grand tenor. Perhaps that was why I was attracted to him.

He leaned against the kitchen counter, sipping his coffee, smiling at me with that dazzling smile, all dark skin and dark beard, like a Middle Eastern movie star, waiting for me to make the first move. Maybe he was intimidated. David, too, would lean against walls, against doorjambs, against bedposts, and look at me with a half-smile, offering himself to me. Do with me what you wish.

Take me. I am yours. I had never wanted a man so much since David. That open invitation was devastating.

I came to him. He put the cup down.

Shall we rip each other's clothes off? he asked ironically. Or rhetorically.

I pressed my body against his. I could feel how big he was though the fabric of his cargo shorts.

I'm hard.

I know.

I took his hand, and we went to my bedroom. There was a bookcase outside the door with all my novels, in English and in translation, stacked on the shelves. He picked up the memoir I had written about the end of my marriage with David, twelve years earlier. It had a big, glamorous photo of me on the cover, black and white. It's me, I said, although it was obvious. He studied the photo for a moment and read the blurbs, then put the book back without saying anything. His face blank. For a second, I wondered if he compared my book cover photo, the one my agent had said made me look like a "glamour-puss," to me now. I didn't think I had changed that much, and I let that fleeting thought go. In my bedroom, he looked around, taking it all in, the mirrors, the antique dresser, all the windows. With an air of calm detachment.

The light was too bright for a first time.

In full daylight, the first kiss. Without the help of darkness, soft lighting, conversation to soften the edges. Like a shot of vodka, neat. His lips, deliciously pulpy. He was skinny, with a slightly hairy chest, narrow shoulders, a soft stomach, not a gym body, but that body felt like fire between my arms.

I collapsed on the bed under him, and he helped me out of my jeans. I was wearing black socks. He put his hand on mine as I was about to peel them off.

No. Keep them.

There was no foreplay, just him inside of me, filling me up so hard I wasn't sure I could take him all in, afraid he would chafe the tender skin inside. And then, as he moved ever so slightly, as his eyes searched mine, something gave way in me, and I dissolved around him.

You're so wet, he whispered, and his face went soft, his breath came faster.

We were not ripping each other's clothes off. There was a slow deliberateness to his moves. A shyness, even, as though he was waiting for a signal from me to let loose. He was elusive, withholding, as if he had been detached from his body, his mind floating above us, watching ironically. And the chemistry between us was so intense I could barely abandon myself. My body was trembling, holding back from fear of being consumed. One time, many years ago, I had smoked *sinsemilla* with David during a trip to the Florida Keys, and while we drove on one of the bridges headed to Key West, I had hallucinated a higher power, a God watching me from the sky. This felt like a high too, but a high that was more emotional than purely sexual. I came in long, almost silent sighs, just before him. I leaned against his chest and touched him gently where his sex was resting on top of his thighs.

I am not a good rebound guy, he apologized. Not like when I was twenty-five.

I was touched he worried about not living up to my expectations. I wanted to take him in my arms, to reassure him. Instead, I teased him.

You aren't so young anymore. Thirty-seven is practically middle-aged.

I had forgotten my own age, by then. I was just the right age. Or no age at all. Age was but a number.

I ran my fingers through the hair that curled on his chest.

Hmmm. So soft.

I put lotion on it, he joked. L'Occitane.

L'Occitane? That's a French brand. How come you know about it?

Men who live in New York can't help being metrosexual, he said.

It was funny to be so attracted to a guy who labeled himself a metrosexual. Also a jazz guitarist. When I was a teenager, my crushes *had* been musicians: Liszt, Chopin, Schubert, Beethoven. I played their music on the piano, the same one that was now in my living room, and I listened to their albums on my little orange turntable. But they were all dead. A few days after Jonah's visit, while doing research on a book I was working on, I randomly opened one of my earlier novels, and was astonished to discover that the heroine's boyfriend was a guitarist and that her ex-husband and the father of her daughter was a musician. I had completely forgotten about it. I never reread my books after they were published. It was as though I had hallucinated them. But these coincidences happened a lot in my life. I'd create a character, and then the real life counterpart appeared, as if I had manifested them unconsciously.

He got up. He couldn't stay. He had to go to work. Men, always busy, always running from one activity to the next, all action. Buttoning his shirt over his T-shirt. Pulling on his shorts. I had lost all sense of time. I took him to the door and stood in front of him, naked except for the knee-high socks.

I watched him cross the landing, guitar case on his back, in shorts and flip-flops (it was a warm day). In a flash, I remembered David in his flannel shirts and ripped jeans, the very incarnation of the eternal American sexy boy. And then that other flash: David, just back from the redeye, walking up these same stairs with the bag he had taken to LA to meet his lover. All night I had prepared myself to ask him to leave. All night I had repeated the words: It's over. You need to leave. You need to leave now. *Now.* Furious to have been caught red-handed, he had mashed the fedora he had taken to wearing lately back on his head and bolted for the door, didn't even put the bag down. He only turned back on the landing for a final goodbye with these cryptic words, "You and I are still us."

The *us* of the past, presumably. Because the present *us* was dissolving at that very moment.

Jonah waved at me from the stairs with a smile that was a bit lopsided, tender, with a dash of smirk, a dollop of irony, erasing the last image of David.

To be continued, he said.

6

THE INTERNET WAS full of pictures of him, in concert, at gigs, sexy or silly, clips and videos on his website. I pored over each one of them, trying to unlock his mystery. He had all the accouterments of the Brooklyn musician: the longish hair, the week-old beard, the Vans, the Converse, the work boots, the worn military jacket, the nonchalance. On some of them he was wearing a straw trilby, tipped back. Even worn ironically it made me cringe. Such a hipster look. Flashbacks of David with his fedora, determined to haunt me. I kept digging deeper, stalkerish. It didn't take me long to find Jonah's father. He was a psychiatrist in Tel-Aviv. Blazer over open-collared shirt, severe round glasses. I was surprised, since Jonah had told me he grew up in Seattle. Unfortunately, no matter how much I dug, what flimsy thread I followed, I couldn't find his mother. She lived somewhere in California, in the Bay area. Perhaps under her maiden name. Too bad. Mothers can reveal so much about their son.

There was a photo of him playing with a klezmer orchestra, younger, shaved, with short hair, in three-quarter profile, beautiful, reserved, and focused. A long, sensitive face. A good, serious boy. All that was missing was the yarmulke. He reminded me of David's young cousins that I had met at his family's weddings and funerals.

7

JANUARY 1, 1985. New York City. Upper West Side. A tiny walkup in the seventies on a block teeming with drug dealers. A New Year's Day party. I barely know these people. I've come with a friend who knows them. I am living in Montreal, then, where I moved after college. Everyone sitting on pillows, a joint passed around. He slides next to me, leaning on one elbow. Lean, reddish, curly hair, beard. His accent reminds me of Woody Allen, the only New York Jew I'm familiar with, although for a few minutes he pretends he's Irish, ha-ha. I may be French, but I've got a good ear for languages and he can't keep the pretense very long. We crack up. He makes experimental movies. I've just published my first book of poetry, although my ambition is to write novels. That night I follow him to his digs on Morningside Heights.

It's what they call love at first sight. Or is that lust? I can't tell the difference, even now. Lust is the only thing that's tangible. We don't leave the bed for twenty-four hours and the next night way past midnight we go roaming the streets of the Upper West Side for a joint open twenty-four seven. We are starved. He's a heavy weed smoker, but at least his years shooting H in college are far behind him. Anyway, I don't know anything about his past that night.

For me he's home. The home I never had. He becomes the port in my life. I never call him my husband. He's David. My man. My guy. Later, after Juliet is born, we find this apartment where I still live in Alphabet City. I buy it cash for a pittance thanks to a small inheritance from my grandfather, at a time when the neighborhood is so run down and destroyed that half the buildings can be bought by paying off the landlords' parking tickets. When David leaves, twenty-two years later, the apartment remains my anchor. The family home. I can't even consider ever moving.

8

WE MESSAGED BACK and forth on the site the next couple of days, and he texted me on Wednesday afternoon.

Will you be home at 6?

My heart leapt. He was brash, impulsive. And I liked it, I liked that brashness, that impetuousness.

Guitar lesson was cancelled, he said, hanging his jacket on a hook in my hallway, dropping off his guitar carefully against the dining room table, making himself at home. I just can't stay very long. I have a concert in the evening.

That's okay, I said. I'm going to an opening later.

It was darker this time in my room, my bed half in shadow and a splash of light in the mirror that trailed across the wood floor and bisected the comforter. We stood in front of the mirror, him lifting my sweater from behind. My breasts popped out of my bra, and he brushed my nipples with the tips of his fingers. They immediately stood stiff, upright, and I started breathing hard. I took his hand and led him to the bed, but we didn't take the time to get fully undressed. He entered me right away.

You were so ready for me, he whispered, his lips on my lips, my skirt pushed up to my waist. My legs naked around his thin hips. He kissed me ardently in a way he hadn't the first time. But afterward, when I rolled down from under him and ran my fingers through his beard, searching his eyes, I immediately sensed a distance, like a denial of the kiss.

He turned towards me, and said: You know I can't stay late, apologetic again.

I know. You told me. It's fine.

His hand trailed on my shoulder over the strap of the t-shirt that I was still wearing, landed awkwardly on my naked thigh. I leaned my whole body against him and he gathered me in his arms and we stayed like this without speaking, stunned by the intensity of what had just happened.

I like your place, he said, looking around my room. It feels like a home.

I took his hand in mine. Inside his left wrist was a small tattoo in Hebrew. I imagined his brown, nervous fingers so sensitive because they touched his guitar, they caressed the strings, they pulled and plucked them. I wanted them inside of me. I placed his hand between my legs. He didn't say anything but left his hand cupping me, gently caressing me, while I asked him about his music. He was part of a group of experimental jazz players. He loved John Zorn, John Lurie, the Lounge Lizards. Jim Jarmusch. Oh my God, I said, the *Down by Law* soundtrack. I know. John Lurie's sax!

I told him I used to go to the Wooster Group and see Spalding Grey, listen to the Lounge Lizards at the Knitting Factory, John Zorn at Tonic, hang out at CBGB and see Blondie, Sonic Youth, The Talking Heads. I played up my 80s street creds at the risk of reminding him of my age, but he seemed genuinely interested. I told him about the poetry magazine, the readings we organized in the far East Village—the Lower East Side as we used to call it—in dive bars tucked between shooting galleries, when you had to thread your way in the middle of the night through groups of junkies sweating, waiting for the next delivery of Black Stripe, Toilet, Royal Flush, Bull Dog, or ten dollars worth of Body Bag or DOA, or avoid confrontation with a crackhead brandishing a gun to fend off imaginary enemies. How David used to keep a baseball bat under his pillow. The shootouts in the street. Needle Park in Tompkins Square.

Wow, he said, in awe, as though listening to tales of war.

I couldn't see him, the self-proclaimed metrosexual, playing cowboy in the old New York City blighted nights. The new New York City nights didn't hold a candle to the old ones. But in his own way, he owned the night, with his guitar strapped to his back, the late gigs, the all-night recording sessions, jamming way out in Bushwick or Ridgewood, until daybreak. What I imagined, anyway.

The 80s were his roots, like the French *Nouvelle Vague* was mine. I liked that connection between us. Antonioni, Fellini, Godard, Truffaut. French and Italian movie stars of that period. Catherine Deneuve? He shook his head. No. Monica Vitti. I liked his answer. Catherine Deneuve was an ice queen, Monica Vitti was smoldering.

We talked for a little while longer, and then he asked me if he could take a shower, and I listened to the water soothingly streaming in the adjacent bathroom, adding to my state of euphoria. He came out naked, his brown body long and skinny, youthful, more youthful than he should be at his age—but of course, from my perspective, thirty-seven was still very youthful—toweling himself, quickly getting dressed. When I told him I was going to an art opening in Chelsea later, he made a face. What? What's wrong with Chelsea? The art world? The money, he said. I've played at openings there. I don't like the vibe.

The artist is a friend, I said.

Are you going to get dolled up, he asked me as he left, picking up his guitar case, perhaps imagining what I would wear. I liked that we were both going off into the world doing our own thing. I thought about my outfit as I took him to the door, mentally picking clothes that might turn him on, even if he wouldn't be there to see me.

9

OCTOBER 1 WAS Louise's moving day. She had finished her senior year in college in June, spent the summer at home in New York, and just started her first job, doing social media for a tech company in Greenpoint. Her dream was to become an actress. The job was to support her while she took drama classes and acted in small productions. She was going to be sharing a loft in Bushwick with two roommates, on a block of converted industrial warehouses. That week I had to turn Jonah down a couple of times when he wanted to come over. He didn't weigh much in the balance, compared to the enormity of helping Louise start a new life and reassuring her everything would be fine. Not to mention David had announced he couldn't help financially anymore. His commitment had been through Louise's college years. After that, if I wanted to help, I was on my own.

The Sunday of the move, while the moving van waited outside the building, Louise was lying on her bed at home, curled in a fetal position, refusing to budge. It's a bad idea, she kept repeating, pulling the comforter over her head, I am not ready to do this. I should stay home. I am not feeling it.

She is bundled in her hoodie, like a tortoise in its shell, waiting for me to slow down, stop running around, stop making sure everything is ready. She wants things to stand still, for time to freeze, maybe even rewind. What an idea to move to her own apartment, to start her adult life. But even wrapped in her comforter, Louise is observing me. Louise, the undercover spy, notices my moods, takes notes on my posture, the noises I make when I eat, the clothes I wear, monitors my visits to Facebook, to Instagram, as though her job was to keep me on the straight and narrow, for fear I'll fall off an imaginary wagon or vanish into thin air. Mom, she says, you're on Facebook too much. Mom, your hair is getting white. Mom, what's your plan for your old age? Are you going to stay in this apartment, without an elevator? Are we going to die here? It feels like David has been vengefully reincarnated in lovely, ravishing female form—the David of the end, who, having adored me for more than a decade, worshipping me as a poetic and sex goddess for years (or so I thought), shapeshifted and turned against me as I stood in the way of his freedom.

As I forcefully march Louise down the stairs, I'm overcome with guilt. I wonder if mother birds feel the same when they push their offspring off the nest. I left home as soon as I could after college. At twenty-two, I was alone in New York, already safe from all of them on the other side of the Atlantic. Home was too toxic.

I've rented a man with a van for the move, to carry Louise's boxes and suitcases and a few pieces of furniture we have bought for her at the little antique store down the block.

The driver is balding with a blondish-grey ponytail and thick silver rings on his fingers. He looks about my age. The van is banged up, and there's a bunch of electric equipment at the back, which he pushes to make room for our boxes and furniture.

I'm a musician, he says, hopping into the van. Always carrying things around.

What instrument?

Guitar. Keyboard too. But mostly guitar.

What kind of music?

Bit of everything, jazz, folk. Rock.

I imagine him as a dashing young guitarist with flowing locks. Now he seems worn out. Music is a hard life. He has trouble helping us carry the chest of drawers up the steps of Lulu's building. Will Jonah be like this in twenty years? Using a van to move furniture around to make ends meet, or will he be able to pull it off as a musician? Unless he becomes a recording engineer and just gigs on the side? Or he finds a solid, successful wife, like David has, to support his music? Would I still be attracted to him then? The man with the van is out of breath when we finish taking everything up. I write a check to him, and he takes a CD out of his glove compartment and hands it to me. My latest guitar recording, he says. I thank him, then forget about it and never listen to it.

The text from Jonah pops up while I am on the subway on my way back from Brooklyn.

How did the move go?

I am touched, grateful even, that he remembered the big day. I can feel my guard slip down, my heart open up a little, to this boy who may have marched carelessly into my life with no other intention than to fuck me, and just as casually inserted himself into my real life, the one I live offline.

Me: Not easy.

Him: A lot of heavy lifting?

Me: Yes. That too. But mainly a lot of emotional lifting. I told Louise she would have two homes, that she would always be home at my place.

Him: Exactly. I like the idea of two homes.

Me: Where would your second home be?

Him: Kyoto.

Me: Have you ever been there?

Him: No.

Me: My other home is Paris. In some ways, it's more my home than New York.

He doesn't respond to my comment about Paris, which, to be honest, I threw in just to catch his attention. I'm not even sure it's still true. Paris is where I come from, the white villa in the posh western suburbs, with the chestnut trees mounting guard by the gate, the wisteria dripping from the porch, the rose bushes, the ivy climbing up the façade, the antique furniture and the thick carpets, all the better to absorb the screams and slammed doors, the curses and insults, the silences and sidelong glances. To bury the secrets.

And yet. Paris is my imaginary refuge when things get tough in New York, with its sidewalk cafés and narrow, pebbled streets, hidden gardens. When David left, my first impulse was to call international schools and look for apartment rentals in Paris. The frenzy lasted about a month, until I came back to my senses. France has made me, but going back is an illusion. Only ghosts are waiting for me there and, worst of all, my own ghost, the little *bastard* girl, ashamed of having no father, ashamed of her wild, reckless mother.

Later in the evening, when I am back home, I invite him to come over. He lives in East Williamsburg, near Bushwick, on the G line, not an easy commute, but he has a car.

Can't, unfortunately. I'm playing tonight.

I am disappointed. It would have been the perfect evening to have him over and celebrate my newfound freedom. For a second, I think of asking him to come after his gig, but that would feel pushy, interfering with his musician's life. Although I have no basis on which to found that idea, I sense that work is an easy excuse for him to get out of any commitment or involvement.

Alone in the apartment, I water my plants, which have thrived over the summer in the humid New York heat and bright light. I pour a half-saucer of dry cat food and a fresh bowl of water for Kiki, who's been rubbing her soft fur against my ankle to remind me she was hungry. Then I sit on the floor of my study, cross-legged, watching the sky turn pink, then translucent blue. It's still warm, but the days are shortening, Fall falling on the city. Darkness coming. Louise's presence fading, leaving behind a bittersweet emptiness, taking a part of our past with her. It's been four years since Vadik vanished in the depth of Kenya, four long, dry years, only interrupted by a couple of brief, forgettable affairs. My nose to the grindstone, focused on making sure Louise had everything she needed at college, religiously splitting the bills with David, trying to write. All that mattered to me was that Louise, who had difficult teenage years, would adjust to college and to life away from home. I had put aside any thoughts of relationships.

When Juliet left home for good after college, she went straight to Bushwick to live with her boyfriend from college. Bushwick, where all the boomers' children end up. I was thrilled for Juliet, who was starting her new life. Louise was still at home. The two of us sailing blindly through the New York choppy waters on our own. David had been the family pillar. He was the domestic one, the cook, the disciplinarian, while I played second fiddle, focusing on my books and articles, my teaching. I had more moneymaking work than he had. But I also didn't trust myself. My mother had been largely absent from my upbringing, at least as a mom. The mom tasks were done by my grandmother; and David, who had grown up with brothers and sisters and a multitude of cousins in the same household. He was a natural. Tacitly the tasks between us had been sorted out. He was a loving father despite his temper. When he left, I panicked. How could I be a mother and a breadwinner at the same time? The fear of facing the day-to-day alone with Louise was such that I barely allowed myself to grieve.

I go to Louise's room and sit on her bed. The room is a war zone of clothes discarded on the floor around the bed, shoes kicked this way and that, and books tumbling off the shelves. The IKEA desk is a battleground of old SAT books, college textbooks, folders of college papers, plays, DVDs, CDs, and mangy teddy bears. I lie down on the bed and pull the comforter, still faintly smelling of Louise's perfume, over my head. In a few minutes, I fall into a deep sleep.

I wake up in the middle of the night and see a woman in a long white nightgown walk into the half-open door. It's the kind of nightgown my mother used to buy in vintage shops, after Juliet was born and she decided she was going to be a respectable grandmother. She stocked up on Victorian embroidered nightgowns, proper little linen dresses, and shoes with stacked heels. When I saw her waiting for us at the Nice airport in her Laura Ashley dress, I thought, what did this woman do to my mother? It didn't last. After a few days in the heat of the summer in Provence, she was back in her hippie caftans and rope sandals. But she went on sleeping in the lacy nightgowns.

I sit up, holding my breath. She looks translucent under the thin cotton. It's not a dream. I am awake. I could reach out with my hand and touch her. Hovering by the door for a few seconds, she takes a few steps within the room, heads straight for the bed, hesitates, then pivots and vanishes at the door. Was she looking for Louise? Did she have a message to pass on to her? Had she come to say goodbye? She passed away ten years ago, almost to the day.

The ethereal shape silently slips out of the door. I am alone now. Louise is gone. Louise, who has been my constant companion since the divorce, the two of us way too tightly entwined, clinging to each other. A bumpy, intense ride. The nightly ritual of reading a book to Louise, her tiny body resting into the crook of my arm. The frightening teenage years. The college years. Endless years. Abruptly ended.

Maybe Louise is right, maybe she wasn't ready to move into her own life. If that's the case, it's on me. I haven't known how to reassure her, how to boost her self-confidence, how to make her feel secure after David left. I remember how happy she was, a dreamy, imaginative little girl dancing in the old videotapes David made of her at her first birthday parties, her arms akimbo and collapsing in giggles. I bury my face in a pillow and weep. The weight of the empty apartment spreads around me, still bristling with the past.

10

BARRY10013, 28, I bet we would have fun together ;)

Loverbabe81, 32 – You have a really strong "energy" to your profile.

Roger-taco, 45 – You have a great aesthetic. Also, you write in complete sentences. You're an anomaly on this site.

BobRedford, 36 – Would you like to go out with a young stud like me?

Jon420, 49 – Would you really be interested in a guy just cause he's well endowed?

11

MONDAYS AND WEDNESDAYS are the days Jonah goes to the recording studio, a few blocks down Avenue B, where he works as a sound engineer, and also manages and books the sessions. I work at home at my freelance translation, which I ironically call my "day job." I translate into French and rewrite the website of a major US fashion designer, pushing my actual writing to the evening hours.

In the afternoon, when he's at the recording studio, we both log on the site, in a kind of unspoken rendezvous. The band above the little chat window on the side of my screen pops hot pink whenever someone types a new message. My screen is covered by half a dozen windows overlapping, the software platform window on which I work, the English-French dictionary window, the email window, the designer website opened in Chrome, Google opened in Safari. We spin kinky scenarios taking place on my bed, in his office, in my study, in my kitchen or my living room, in the backroom of seedy dive bars.

But sometimes, I leave the chat window open and he doesn't come on. I know when he's online because of the little green dot next to his picture. I watch it, hoping he'll stroll by and say hey, but time passes, and the green dot keeps its vigil near his pic. It's like being at a party and the guy you've been sleeping with shows up and gives you the cold shoulder and talks to other girls, and you die of humiliation—wait, maybe there's a glitch. What if he left the window open and forgot to log out?

Yeah, right! He's online for sure, checking girls, sending messages, flirting, browsing profiles, ignoring me. I feel a pinch of unjustified jealousy. I watch him silently from behind the screen of my computer. Of course, if he cared to check up on me, he would see *my* little green dot and assume I was reading messages, flirting, browsing, both of us playing the virtual field. The difference is that he most likely doesn't even notice my green dot, or perhaps wouldn't even care if he did.

Thursday-Sunday, he's on the other side of the river, in *his* real life. On his website, he's sitting behind a table with a guitar on his lap, a sunny window to the side, with a ledge covered in succulents and tropical flowers and a tall rubber plant leaning in a corner. Behind him, electrical equipment and musical instruments are piled on shelves. I imagine a loft with a bed in the corner, a bed in which I'd like to spend a night, just once waking up in his arms.

So far, we've only seen each other at my place when he comes to the East Village. A quick text and he pops over after work. His real life seems as unreachable as if he lived on the side of the Atlantic. The first time he came over, he had mentioned inviting me to his place, but he never brought it up again, and the possibility now seems remote, like a vanishing mirage. Sometimes we chat when he's at home working on some recording, and his existence becomes all the more tantalizing because I can't touch it or be part of it.

12

IT WAS LATE October. He had been coming two or three times a week since we'd met, and the sex was so good I allowed myself to relax. Who cared if it was an affair or a romance? One afternoon he got off work early and came straight from the studio and even though he had warned me, as he usually did, that he couldn't stay late, he accepted my offer of espresso. I thought his warnings were a kind of preemptive announcement, in case he needed an exit strategy, like when he had offered to meet me just before work the first time. But perhaps I had it wrong. Perhaps he merely didn't want to disappoint me in promising more than he could deliver.

We were lying on my bed, facing each other, our legs entwined, after making love, when he asked me if I had seen Haneke's *Amour*. Dusk was falling. If it had been a French movie from the sixties, Godard's *Vivre Sa Vie,* for instance, or Agnès Vardas's *Cléo de Cinq à Sept,* the scene would be shot in black and white, the lighting making our skin velvety with deep shadows, and we'd both be smoking a cigarette.

No, I said. I didn't. I didn't want to see it. I was afraid it would be too painful.

I remembered my grandmother watching a movie on TV one day and there was a scene with a train speeding head-on into the frame. She started to scream in terror, jumping out of her chair, terrified the train was about to run her over. She was in her mid-nineties, perhaps an acceptable age to go senile, but imagine it happening to you.

Oh no. It's beautiful. The love they share is incredibly touching.

I was surprised. He was always so ironic and detached I didn't expect him to reveal that kind of vulnerability. That he was the kind of boy who could be touched by an old couple still deeply in love moved me so much my heart melted. One day he would meet a woman he would love and marry and perhaps spend the rest of his life with. And I'd never be that woman for him. If we were closer in age… perhaps it was a delusion, but I was sure it would be love between us. It was unmistakable, the way my whole body was dissolving with tenderness. And the gentle, searching look he had in his eyes when he looked at me. I felt my face soften with regret.

What?

I shook my head. Nothing. Go on.

Okay. Here's another one I love. A Thai filmmaker. Nobody can remember his name. "*Uncle Boonmee Who Can Recall His Past Lives.*" Funny title, right? Check it out. Just google Thai filmmaker.

Have you always loved movies?

My brother turned me on when I was like ten or twelve. He's ten years older than me. So, he'd come back from college for the summer, and we'd watch everything on VHS cassettes. All the French *nouvelle vague*, the Thai movies, the Korean movies, the more obscure the better. I had the most extensive film education for a ten year old!

Bet it messed you up forever!

Ha! You're probably right.

How about Wong Kar-Wai?

In the Mood for Love? Loved it. But when it came out I was older.

You're a romantic.

I thought it was hot.

Okay.

I shot him a look like I still believed he was romantic, and he gave me a little teasing kick in the shin. Then I asked him if he had seen *2046*.

What's that?

Another Wong Kar-Wai. I can't believe you don't know about it.

He laughed. Sorry to disappoint you!

So good. Most of it takes place in that motel in the 60s. Super sultry and weird. Vaguely science-fiction. Hot too.

He leaned forward and kissed me full on the lips.

I watched the Thai movie after he left. The tropical setting, the slow scenes, the mysterious sensuality made me think of him, of his music. The clips I had watched of his quartet had a distinct Asian tempo, perhaps because of the extensive use of the oud. A few days later, he texted me he'd checked out Wong Kar-Wai's *2046* after seeing *Gravity*, the Alonso Cuarón's science-fiction movie everyone was talking about. And that he'd liked *2046* so much better. He added a heart emoji.

In my dog-eared copy of Ovid's *The Art of Love*, I had underlined this passage, way before it was relevant to me:

"Women who are getting on in years have experience, and it is only experience that sets the seal of perfection on our natural gifts… No pictured representation can rival them in voluptuousness. With them pleasure comes naturally, without provocation, the pleasure which is sweeter than all, the pleasure which is shared equally by the man and the woman… Let who will hasten to drink new and immature wine. Let me have a rich mellow vintage dating back to one of our elder consuls. It is only after many years that the plane tree affords a shelter from the scorching sun, and fields but newly reaped hurt the naked foot… If you would enjoy the fruits of love in their maturity, you will obtain, if only you persevere, a reward worthy of your desires."

13

THE CHAT BOX glowed hot pink.

Salut! Ça va? (I had taught him a few French words).

My heart leapt. I didn't expect to hear from him on a Sunday afternoon.

He: *Will you be there at 6? I want to bend you over your piano.*

Me: *You'd have to come earlier. Louise is coming for dinner.*

Two hours later, he cancelled. He had to substitute for a friend and give a guitar lesson. I felt a sting of disappointment, but then I remembered the heart emoji he had texted me after watching the Wong-Kar Wai movie, and my chest melted a little bit at his impulsiveness.

You spend way too much time on that site, Louise said in a stern voice, hearing the ping of a new message on my phone. She was home from Brooklyn for our Sunday night menu of takeout Indian food, *Game of Thrones* and *GIRLS*. I quickly made Jonah's latest text vanish from the screen.

I get messages. I gotta log on and answer them.

Louise picked up my phone and scrolled through the apps. She rolled her eyes in horror.

Mom! No! I can't even…NOT Tinder! You can't go on Tinder. It's for 16-year-olds.

I was pulling off the zip on my boots, the same clog-boots with the wooden soles that Jonah had told me he liked when we first met.

I know this woman—an art dealer—who met someone on Tinder when she was traveling for work in Chicago, I said, and now they are dating. She's 46.

46 is not elderly like you, Louise deadpanned, helping herself from chicken *tika marsala* and *saag* spinach.

At what age does elderly start?

I don't know. Like 55?

I kicked off the boots, pushed them under the coffee table and sat cross-legged on the couch, my plate balanced on my knees, trying to absorb the blow. Louise pulled the blanket over us and clicked on *Game of Thrones*. We watched Tyrion Lannister and Daenerys Targaryen engage in a verbal joust while our respective dishes of chicken masala and vegetable kumai gave off a scrumptious aroma.

You guys are much more conservative than we are, I said, soaking a piece of poori into the bright orange masala sauce. Our generation broke a lot of rules. Age means nothing to me. I want to enjoy the years that I still have ahead of me.

An expression of panic passed in Louise's eyes. You're in denial. You're not getting any younger, you know. I won't be able to take care of you when you're old. Who's going to take care of you when you can't climb the stairs?

Well, there's Juliet and Scott. I giggled. I can move in with them. My grandmother climbed the stairs in her house when she was in her 90s. I'm not there yet. But anyway, I can sell the apartment and move to a place with an elevator, or better yet find a young, muscular guy to carry me up and down the stairs?

Mom!

I was kidding, *mon amour*. But what do you want me to do? I am not going to live with any man, just because. I was married with your dad for twenty-two years. It's not easy to start over with someone else. I wanted to be free for a while.

For a while? That was almost thirteen years ago!

I got up and wrapped my arms around her shoulders.

Ma chérie. Maybe I haven't found the right man to settle down with.

Stop it. Louise moved her shoulders this way and that to get rid of the hug like a dirty blanket. You won't find him on Tinder, that's for sure! And don't stand in front of the TV!

When I opened my phone the next morning, the Tinder icon had disappeared. I let it go. I was on another dating app. Anyway, I'd never even gone on Tinder. I'd just downloaded it out of curiosity.

After David's departure, I turned into the merry widow, dancing until the wee hours on the roofs of Williamsburg when it was still industrial no man's land, hanging out in the Lower East Side dive bars, flirting with the boys at Saturday night parties in East Williamsburg and Bushwick, dating a couple of screenwriters friends of David's who suddenly showed their interest. Men are loyal to their men friends until the coast is clear. I had my weekends free while Louise spent them with her dad and his new wife. It was like being twenty again. With David, I thought I had the couple and the family of my dreams. I disregarded the fights, his bad moods, his reproaches. His fits of anger. My panic attacks. I thought I had found my dream life.

I'm watching them, crouched on the first floor landing, with a plunging view of the front hall, the front door banging. My grandparents are waiting to ambush my mother. It's late, and she's just come back from the last metro, tiptoeing on her bare feet, her shoe straps dangling from her fingers. Where have you been, slut? You should be ashamed of yourself. *Et la petite alors!* You're irresponsible! My mother curses so hard, spit forms at the corner of her mouth. Fuck you, old farts! Dumbasses. I silently tiptoe back to my room so she doesn't see I'm up. I don't want to cause any more drama.

She's a communist at that time. She goes door-to-door, selling an encyclopedia of communist poets to raise money for the PCF, the French Communist Party. She turned over her card when the news started coming from the USSR that it wasn't all it was cracked up to be.

Even later, at sixty, seventy, she's unstoppable, my mother. She looks twenty years younger. She has gay friends, friends of all ages, of all cultures. A hippie. A gypsy. She doesn't act her age, nor her social class. She's as comfortable with truck drivers as with artists or politicians. She hates the *bourgeoisie.* She drives her camping-car all over the world, her white kayak perched on the roof, braving the rapids, skiing, spending her winters in the far north in an isolated cabin without running water, heated by a stone fireplace, until she dies in her late 80s, just back from a final trip across Europe. A force of nature. A real *mec*, people say—a *dude*. They can't fathom that a woman who travels the world, who curses like a sailor, who sleeps alone under the stars, who's one of the guys, is a real woman. She has balls. A bombshell, with the heart of an adventurer. She's not much of a mother, my mother. I am angry at her for years, ashamed of her for flaunting all the conventions. But she's the freest woman I ever met.

14

I PULLED A Heineken from the fridge. I'd grabbed the pack at the deli the day before, just for his visit, because I don't usually keep beer in my apartment.

Heineken, so *80s*, he teased me, taking a swig. Smiling his dazzling smile.

The next time he came, I made sure to get a proper, Brooklyn-brewed IPA.

You didn't have to do that. He pointed to the Brooklyn Lager label. Heineken was fine. I was joking.

I know, I said. But I was embarrassed he had so easily seen through me.

We were seated on my big couch, our legs touching, sharing the bottle of IPA. He placed his hand on my thigh, and it was like an electric burst flashing through my body.

Wow, you still have the old tapes! With his other hand, he pointed to the shelves sagging under the weight of the VHS and audiocassettes that had continued to live there, gathering dust, after David's departure. Betraying my age, like the unused landline my Wi-Fi was still connected to. I felt my cheeks turn hot, and I vowed to get rid of the tapes and the old bookcase, everything that was left over from David.

Bit by bit, Jonah had been telling me about himself. He had studied music at Berklee and moved to New York after 9/11 and gotten into the experimental jazz scene right away. He played with his own quartet—they had produced a CD a couple years ago—but mostly he played as a sideman with various bands and had made records with them as well. The latest one had just come out, and they'd had an event at *Le Poisson Rouge*.

He never said any of this in a bragging tone, but matter of fact, like, that's a musician's life, and I shouldn't be impressed, even though I was, because I knew from my own experience how hard it was to survive and persevere as an artist in New York. He had also scored a couple of movies, including one that had won a prize at Sundance. I only knew about the prize because I'd watched the clips on YouTube. I had really liked the music. I could see he was pleased, and I told him I had mentioned him to one of my screenwriter friends, who was looking for a composer. It was for an indie film, but James Franco was attached, I added, chuckling ironically. It would get made.

He slowly put the bottle down on the table and dropped his hand from my leg.

There was a distinct change in the vibe. I turned toward him.

What? What's the matter?

You told him about…? He swept the air between him and me with his hand, as if he couldn't bring himself to say *us*, as if these two letters would bring us together in an unacceptable bond.

Her. Not him. My friend Lena. Why?

My brother… Hmm… He's a director. I wouldn't want him to find out.

My heart sunk.

I wouldn't want him to find out. So that's why he didn't want any public dates with me. Not *because I had already decided* but because he only wanted to see me on the DL. I was the woman with the scarlet letter. I knew all about those women. My mother had been that woman, the unmarried mother, the woman with the scandalous love life. The mistress. The woman who trailed a vapor of sulfur behind her, and considered her role on the planet was to burst open hypocrisies, expose the pus, hang the dirty laundry in public, pull out all the shit pushed under the rug.

When my mother got pregnant and started to show, she was shipped to a home in Brittany for unwed mothers until I was born. Then we all moved to the big villa outside Paris with my grandparents, and my mother got a fake wedding ring she slipped on her left hand to pretend she was married, even though all her mail was addressed to *Mademoiselle*, which filled me with shame. My father was in med school, and disappeared midway through the pregnancy, when his parents found out my mother was ten years older. A tart prying on his naiveté. Not a pure young thing. Who even knew if he really was the father?

He was nervous, sipping on his IPA, avoiding my eyes. He looked very young, way younger than his age, as if he had suddenly realized I was holding his fate between my hands. I recognized that look on his face. He was *ashamed.* Why? Because he was sleeping with an older woman who could almost be his mother? Because with one word from me I could ruin his image in front of his brother, in front of the whole world? But what image was that? A jazz musician is not exactly a model of straight living. Why would his brother care about who he was dating, sleeping with, or fucking? What power did his brother have over him, what image was he trying to give his older brother that he was so worried about destroying it with a naughty misalliance?

And then it dawned on me.

Wait, your brother is… Judd Burnstein?

Actually I wrote the music for his first two.

Judd Burnstein was famous for his personal, semi-autobiographical movies. I had seen a couple. I tried to remember if there was a younger brother in any of them.

You did? *Swing Left* is my favorite.

I didn't do that one. I did *Baby Girl* and *The Mendelsohn Files.*

Wow. I remember the music for *Baby Girl.* So cool.

I didn't want to keep working for Hollywood. By the time you pay all your musicians, it's barely worth it. Besides… I don't know… Maybe I should give it a shot again. But I don't like that world. It's all about money. It's fake.

He sounded like Louise. *Fake* was her most merciless criticism. Kiss of death.

I picked up the bottle and sipped a little from it. I wondered if he felt more exposed because his brother was a hot, up-and-coming director or because he was in competition with him? Did he drop out of Hollywood because he didn't feel he could win the contest?

Or was it truly that world of money he hated, just as he hated Chelsea and the art world? In the silence, desire between us was spreading like a vapor encircling us. But the vapor had turned cold for me, my heart frozen in its center, even though my crotch was liquefying, my underwear soaked. Perhaps his moment of shame aroused me because shame in my family always implied sex, and vice versa. He took the bottle from my hands and set it on the coffee table.

It used to be a tradition, in some circles in France—perhaps only in literature—for young males to be initiated to the delights of sex by a sensually accomplished, older woman. They were much sought after as sexual mentors. Evidently Jonah didn't know that. But I had no reason to give in to his scruples.

I decided to let it go and took his hand.

I felt like the countess in Vivant Denon's eighteenth century novella *No Tomorrow,* taking the young narrator to her boudoir while he imagines unfathomable delights. Or like Lea in Colette's novel *Chéri*—the fifty-year-old ex-*courtisane* who has an affair with the twenty-five-year-old son of her best friend.

In real life, in 1920, at the age of forty-seven, Colette first met the sixteen-year-old son of her husband, Bertrand de Jouvenel, at her seaside villa. Not bothered a bit by society's disapproval, she gave him a copy of her recent novel *Chéri* , with the inscription "*A mon fils chéri, Bertrand de Jouvenel*" ("to my cherished son Bertrand de Jouvenel"). Soon after, they embarked on an intense affair that lasted four years and continued after Colette and her husband divorced.

Am I too forward? I asked, as I led him to my bedroom.

No. Am I?

No. You are the man.

To be honest, he didn't act much like *the man.* But that's what was exciting, the blurriness of the roles, the taboo we were breaking by reversing the conventional order of things. He acted way younger than his age. He seemed almost shy, out of his depth. He handed me the reins. *What will you teach me,* he texted me before coming. *What shall we do now*? It was a kind of vertigo. I felt empowered, and the power was firing me up.

When we got to my room, he took the lead. He pressed me against the wall and took me straight up, my dress pulled up to my waist, my thighs clasping his waist, until we tumbled on the bed, and then he flipped me on my stomach, but not without asking my permission. Metrosexual knight true to the new code of sexual behavior: always ask for consent first.

15

IN THE NOVEL workshop I teach at the New School, we're reading a story by a freshman student, *Trigger Warning.* It's about a date rape, or perhaps not. Or if you were my age you might say, a date that went wrong. The girl's nineteen, the boy two years older. The girl is from Pakistan, fresh off the boat. The boy is from Ohio. The roles are blurry, the signals crossed. There is a slip up. Anal sex. In the story, the author has circled the scene from many angles to try to get to the core of it and make sense of it for herself. The girl is not a victim. The boy is not a perpetrator. Or are they? There's a heated discussion. The reactions are neatly split between the undergrads, all around eighteen or nineteen, and the older students, some in their forties or fifties, who are not taking the class for credit but because they want feedback and deadlines. The first group is horrified. The second, skeptical. One of the students who is in his fifties, a talented writer, doesn't believe there's a rape. Just a bad date, he says. Shit happens.

The classroom is rippling with tension, each generation clinging to its positions. The author, a young woman from southeast Asia, listens in silence, as is the rule during workshop, sitting stoically, her face not betraying her feelings. I try to steer the discussion to the writing itself. Is there a good sense of character? Did the author let the scene unfold without trying to control the reader's reaction?

But they want to debate the heart of the piece, what it means. Was there rape or not? I insist the author herself is not judging her characters. She has captured the scene in its complexity, and that's what makes it good writing. There's no victim and no criminal. The author has explored how boundaries slipped, and how a sexy situation has gotten out of hand. The undergrads look at me with skepticism. That's not what they want to hear. When it's the young author's turn to speak, she thanks the class without adding any interpretation of her own story.

A couple of weeks later, one of the students who had been absent at the last workshop waits for me after class. He's a skinny boy, with an undercut hairstyle and large hazel eyes, almost feverish in his pale face. It's about the piece we discussed, he says. The *Trigger Warning* story. It's not the story so much that upset him, well it *was* upsetting, but the reaction from some of the students. Some of the older guys. He was so shook up, he went to see the nurse and asked to be excused for the rest of the semester.

They didn't realize it was a hot topic, I tell him. They don't see it the same way you guys do. They have a different point of view. They have a different life experience.

I try to convince him to come back, but he stands firm. He's had sort of the same thing happened to him when he was younger, and he got triggered. He really does look pale and shaky. Are you sure? You're going to miss the rest of the semester? He nods. He's already on anti-depressants. I don't insist. I feel sad.

Of course, when I said, "they have a different point of view," I was also thinking of my own. I, too, secretly reacted like my older students. In my generation, girls were ready for the rough and tumble with men. It was so exciting to be free, to have the pill, to do whatever the fuck we wanted, we took it all in stride. We wanted to experience our sexuality like men did. Like an adventure. When I first came to New York at twenty-two, I told myself I was up for anything, except hard drugs. Whatever happened, I would deal with it. I'd take my chances. I liked taking risks, I claimed my feminine power, I owned my mistakes, I never thought I was a victim, even when once or twice, in my twenties, things skidded sideways. Maybe I was lucky. Still, I understand my students, like I try to I understand Louise. We wanted to upset the old world. But they are trying to build a new, better one.

16

AFTER THAT LAST visit, I didn't hear from Jonah. No text, no message on the site. It was the first time I'd had no news from him for more than a week. I had a bad feeling. It was November, the period of the year I found the bleakest ever since David had left, his departure soon followed by my mother's death, the two anchors to my life gone within a few months of each other. Despite all the misgivings I had about my mother, her yearly visit to New York made Thanksgiving and Xmas a true family holiday. It was also in November that I had found out about David's affair after foraging into his credit card statements, devoured by doubt, my denial suddenly lifting, and found an expense for a hotel room in East Hampton one weekend when he was supposed to have gone working on a screenplay with a director friend upstate. I woke him up in the middle of the night and confronted him, the vengeful wife brandishing the incriminating paper in his face.

I ended up sending a message to Jonah on the site, a softer, more casual way to contact him than a phone text. No answer. I forced myself to wait a few more days, then sent another message. Still nothing. I tried to reassure myself. He was erratic, impulsive. Maybe he was touring. I checked his website, like a stalker, and saw only a few concerts in Brooklyn. From what I could tell, he wasn't assiduous about posting his gigs. Perhaps he was out of town.

Still, I panicked at the idea of having lost him.

Austrian scientists have studied the behaviors of people who love bitter food. They discovered they are attracted to rollercoasters, their moods alternate between hot and cold. They put themselves in danger. They are more selfish, cold-blooded. One explanation is that eating bitter food is to play at being scared, because a bitter taste signals a danger to the body. To swallow the food could be dangerous. So you show that you can be strong, a subtle pleasure to boost your self-esteem. Symbolically, it's about defying danger and winning.

Who knew my love for the bitterness of broccoli rabe, the delicate astringency of dandelion greens, the tartness of watercress revealed my urge to live on the edge?

17

LEANING OVER THE long Formica table in the dining room, Alan was working on small canvases, stretching the blue tape diagonally in acute angles and painting the blank areas in broad strokes of black acrylic. When the paint was dry, he ripped out the tape like long Band-Aids and the remaining white lines of canvas created a sharp graphic design in negative in the sea of black. It was like editing down a piece of writing, removing what didn't serve anymore to keep the bare bones.

Alan had stayed with me many times while visiting from Barcelona, where he kept a studio. We had had a brief fling a few years earlier in Warsaw, where we had met, both invited to a mutual friends' wedding, but we had more fun dancing all night, high on Polish vodka than in the narrow bed in which we collapsed out of exhaustion. By the time he came to stay with me in New York, we had become friends. He was English, but he had lived in Barcelona for six years, and was trying to settle in the States with an artist's visa. He had just arrived a week earlier and had already turned one section of my apartment into his studio.

The long, wooden dining room table was now covered with tape, jars filled with brushes, and stacks of paper. He had slipped a large painter's drop cloth under the table to catch the paint drippings and nests of used, coiled tape piling up on the ends of the table and on the floor. He had finished a series of big paintings at a friend's studio, and he was now preparing small canvases for his opening, while listening to *The Cure* on a loop at low volume.

You can turn up the sound, Alan! I'm done with my writing.

Tall, his gray hair clipped short and spiked, he was not only a mordant wit but a good cook. When he was home, he cooked simple vegetarian food he had learnt to prepare in Sicily. He came into the kitchen area and started making dinner. Tonight, was whole wheat pasta with garbanzo beans and broccoli rabe tossed over it.

He was in a kind of on and off romance with an American dancer who had announced to him right off the bat that she "didn't do relationships." Why did Americans—or New Yorkers—put up walls and tried to control the outcome of their affairs? Sitting at the kitchen table across from each other, we talked about the tribulations of our love lives. I had told him about Jonah the first night he'd arrived, and now I wanted to know what he thought of his sudden distance. I liked to hear a man's point of view in these matters. Women often wore rose-colored glasses and tried to spin every man's action in the most favorable light for mutual support or to avoid facing the inevitable, which I had famously done with David. Men read other men better and tell it to you straight.

Alan opened a bottle of Valpolicella and filled two plates with a steaming mix of spaghetti, chickpeas and broccoli rabe, and we sat down to dinner at the kitchen table.

His point of view, after thinking about it for a while, was that *Jazzman* was wishy-washy and didn't know what he wanted, and that maybe, yes, he was ashamed, although it was hard to fathom. Perhaps he came from a religious, orthodox family? We pondered that question for a long time. Why calculate and hedge your bets? Why not just embark and see where it went? Maybe Americans were more risk-adverse than Europeans. As fellow Europeans, we loved to puzzle over the oddities of the natives, in particular the strange puritanism that lurks in the deepest recesses of a society that can be also provocatively raunchy. Or maybe it was a Generation X thing?

In any case, we both agreed I needed another man to take the edge off. The problem is that, since I had signed up on the dating site, I hadn't liked anyone, apart from *Justpassingby* and *Hey11211*. I had had dates with men of all ages, although mostly younger, then invariably turned them down.

There was the hedge fund Turk I had met at a conference about French seduction, whom I turned down after he alluded to the whip and handcuffs he kept in his apartment; the English photographer whose ex-wife was remarried to an ex-con and who gave me a peek at the huge tattoo of an eagle covering his entire upper back; the French IT guy who amused me with his detailed knowledge of women's lingerie (he had a weakness for La Perla and suspender belts) but my attraction didn't survive the walk back to my apartment; the American photojournalist who boasted about the bacon he smoked in his Westchester backyard and offered to be my muse; the married Swedish architect in town for a few days who looked crestfallen that I wasn't interested in the fling he had envisioned; the Jamaican drummer who turned out to have common friends with me on Facebook, where he proudly showed pictures of his newborn baby only a few days after we met. Sometimes the date ended with a kiss at my door, a tongue darting between my lips, before I ran up my stoop and disappeared forever. I knew I was being a tease, leading them on, then shutting them off. Sometimes I canceled the date even before it took place, in a kind of catch-and-release practice.

Alan rolled his eyes. You're not serious, he said, interrupting my long litany.

What do you mean?

You just want to reassure yourself that you've still got it.

Yeah. You're right. But it's easier to find a hookup than a serious guy. It's exhausting, actually. I hate it. I can't stand this sampling of one man after another, like shopping online for dresses and then sending them back. I just want Jonah. If I can't have him, I should just let him go. Online dating is addictive. It's a game. I should be writing instead. The thing is, Jonah inspires me to write. I'm thinking about writing a novella.

Alan refilled our glasses, picked up our plates, and placed them in the dishwasher. I noted how comfortable we were together, like a couple minus the sex we had gotten out of the way early.

That counts for a lot. And I don't think it's a good idea to date defensively.

I am just doing it to protect myself in case Jonah never shows up again. It's lame, I know. Have you ever done it?

What? Dating defensively? I am not American. I don't "date." But yeah. Sure. For a few months, once, I was involved with five different girls. Well… "involved" … Maybe that's not the right word. They would be in a kind of rotation.

Was that defensive?

It was after a breakup. So, yea, in a way.

They each had their turn?

Kind of.

During a period after Vadik, I had seen two men in turns for a few weeks. I liked one more than the other, but I wanted to spare the other one's feelings. In the end, I stopped seeing them both. Five would be hard to juggle. I didn't think I could desire five at the same time. But men multi-tasked better—at least, and perhaps only—as far as women were concerned.

18

VADIK, MY ONLY serious boyfriend after David, was old school: overprotective, reassuring, and jealous. Any mention of a previous lover, including David, was sure to trigger a bout of heavy silence. He worked as an economist at the UN in Geneva. I liked the freedom of a part-time relationship without the confines of living together. And it worked, until he read the manuscript I was writing about the end of my marriage, and he couldn't disguise his distaste, even his sense of betrayal. He offered me a trade-off. I would renounce publishing the book and, in exchange, I would come to Geneva with Louise and he would support us financially. Perhaps, in his mind, he was being a good man, a good provider. Perhaps he thought it was a deal I couldn't refuse. After my mother's death in the south of France the previous year, we had brought back mementos and heirlooms from her house and stored them in his basement locker. When I sensed the end of the relationship with Vadik was near, I asked a cousin who lived on the French side of the border to move it all out.

In the last year of our marriage, I used to call David "Mr. Cool" because he was strutting his stuff, his fedora perched at an angle, in full swagger. He bought a fire engine red Ducati 1200 cc *Monster* and went for long rides up the Taconic or took it for a spin around the Belt Parkway. Or so he said. I thought, oh, he's going through his midlife crisis. It'll pass. I didn't know or didn't want to know there was a woman in the shadows who made him feel like a king, I only sensed something was up, his new demeanor didn't bode well. It took me almost two years to accept that it was over.

19

THANKSGIVING. I REMEMBERED Jonah had a gig early in the week, his own quartet, he had mentioned it when we'd first met and I had seen it on his website, which I was now consulting as often as a booking manager. It was somewhere in Park Slope or Gowanus. For a second, I had an urge to crash his show. Just to see him, convince myself with my own eyes that he still existed, that we still lived in the same reality. But he had traced invisible boundaries around himself that I could only cross at my own peril. Instead, I accepted Lena's invitation to spend the week with her in her cabin in Montauk.

I had known Lena for almost twenty years, when she had approached me to adopt my first novel for the screen. Lena taught screenwriting at NYU and was divorced too—more recently than me. Her ex-husband worked in finance, and she had gotten their beach cabin in the divorce. She also kept an old, beat-up Nissan in a parking lot near the Jitney stop and headed to the beach to write as often as she could. It was a simple cottage, wood paneled, with a retro chintz décor. Musty smelling but when you sat on the deck at sunset, the quiet of a summer evening infused with the scent of honeysuckle and jasmine, the briny smell of the ocean, and the lapping of the waves brought peace even to the most agitated souls.

After unpacking, I showed Lena a picture of Jonah on my laptop, the one where he looked like a Middle Eastern movie star with his curly hair tumbling forward, his stubble of beard, and his soulful eyes. Just looking at that picture made me feel weak.

Oh my God, Lena said. You're doomed.

We opened a bottle of wine and drank up to sexy, doomed, secret affairs. Lena had been online dating for a few months, and we giggled over her latest dates while I filled her in on my affair with Jonah. Together we looked up his website and watched a clip of his quartet. She liked *Ballad for Vida* and thought his music would work as a score for her film.

I told him you were looking for a composer. He had a weird, screwed-up reaction. He was afraid you'd tell his brother about us.

What? Who's his brother?

Judd Burnstein.

No way! Judd Burnstein!! Are you kidding me? Small world.

Of course they knew each other. She had invited him to give a master class to her students. We took our glasses to the deck and sat in rocking chairs, bundled up in blankets. Even though it wasn't the magic of a summer night, it was mild for the end of November and the gentle lapping of the ocean was soothing.

With Lena's validation of his music, I felt proud of Jonah, as if we were together for real, even though I knew I was only borrowing him for a short while. Not only was he beautiful, but he was talented. Here on the deck of the cottage, on a clear night bursting with stars, I imagined him sitting on the beach below, stringing his guitar and joining me later in the musty bed of the guest room. I started to feel the wine, cocooned into a soft haze. Jonah was all the boys I had ever been with, he was David in his Venice Beach cottage off the boardwalk, David on Montego Bay, David when we were the hot, talented couple in the East Village. He was François on San Andrès off the coast of Columbia, Vadik on Porquerolles Island in the Mediterranean where we had spent a week together while I was writing an article for a travel magazine. I stretched my legs and rocked a little in the rattan rocking chair.

Still, the physical distance from New York was a relief. My obsession lost a bit of its grip, and I pledged to avoid checking the dating site for the whole week. In the city, I was so busy with my translation job and my teaching that I usually only had time to do my own work in the evening. It was a rare luxury to have several full days to write. My resolution only lasted two days. On the third day I logged on the site without thinking, my fingers blindly hitting the keys on their own.

I made a mug of tea, and by the time I carried it back to the table where I had set up my laptop, the hot pink band above the chat box was blinking.

Hi Sweetie!

My heart did a double sault. He was on! I hadn't lost him. But *Sweetie*? What was that about? He usually said *Salut* in French. *Hi Sweetie!* sounded… fake… Also, so… American. Of course he *was* American. *Sweetie.* Almost corny. It didn't sound like him either. He would never have said *sweetie* to me in person. What character was he playing? What suave player was he pretending to be?

Never mind. He was on, that was all that mattered. Why quibble on his use of a word? *Hi Sweetie* was… sweet and lovely. In spite of myself, in spite of his recent silence, I felt a burst of tenderness.

He: How are you?

Me: I am in the Hamptons, staying with a friend, writing and biking.

He: Sounds great. I am upstate.

I waited a beat. And then I waited another beat. And then another one.

He was gone. And right away I ached for hm.

His impulsive, unpredictable greetings dotting the chat box were like grains of caviar—or hits on a crack pipe. Always making me want more.

The last night at the beach, the weather abruptly turned wintry, with harsh gusts of wind, too cold to stay outside in the evening. We made a fire in the fireplace.

You better watch out with this guy, Lena said, leaning toward the fireplace with a poker to steady the stack of logs. I've been there. An Italian. Married. We were both married. He was beautiful, too. I couldn't get him out of my brain. For two years. It wrecked me and almost wrecked my marriage. Get out before it's too late.

There was the warning light again flashing in my gut, that sense of danger that morphed seamlessly into excitement. Into desire. I saw his curly hair, his beard, his pale eyes contrasting with his dark skin, that nonchalance he had, walking by without a care in the world, as though he had crossed my path just to remind me of all the boys that I had ever wanted so badly to follow, to snatch me away from my life, to make me discover mysterious delights. His very elusiveness was irresistible.

It became a challenge I needed to win.

20

KNIGHTRIDERETHAN, 32 – You have a really strong "energy" to your profile

OrgasmHunter, 36 – Sorry I have to reschedule

Jonathan, 44, Brooklyn – Hi, I am physically attracted to women 15 to 20 years older than me. Someone between 58-63. 2 or 3 years ago a much older woman started flirting with me and asked me out. Nothing happened but from that day on, I became everyday more attracted to older women. I really have a crush on women in their sixties. The idea of doing something forbidden when dating a much older woman only strengthens my desire for such relationship.

Back home, I click through his pics. Dark hair, sensitive face, soft gray eyes. He doesn't say what he does for work. I figure a musician, a furniture designer, a carpenter. Then I think: another Jonah.

My thumb hovers over his pic, hesitates, then swipes left.

On Facebook a woman has posted a status: *Are 50- and 60-year-old women the new hot babes?* Fifteen women respond that they were only dating thirty-year-olds. One offers an explanation: 1) we are available and game; 2) we don't try to marry them and have babies; 3) we are more sexually experienced and freer; 4) we give good conversation.

In the *New Yorker* opened on my kitchen table, a cartoon shows a stylist, scissors in hand, standing behind a middle-aged woman and asking her: *"age-appropriate or age-defying?"* When I go to the hairstylist, I always pick *"age-defying."*

21

WE HAD ALREADY entered the December tunnel, snow on the ground and Xmas looming ahead with its garland of flickering lights. I hadn't seen him in a month. Since Thanksgiving we had been messaging on and off on the site, dialogue for an endless XXX movie. Each text a promise of bliss, a question mark. *Is the game still on. R u still there? R we still there?* It was nerve-wracking, but I was powerless to resist him.

Hi baby! The band atop my chat box glowed hot pink.

Him: *Are you craving my cock?*

Me: *Don't flatter yourself. I am working by the way. You're interrupting me.*

Him: *You didn't have to answer me ;(*

Me: *Touché! Actually, if you want to know, you press all my erotic buttons.*

Him: *That's exactly what I wanted. Keep you on your toes.*

Me: *Oh yeah? How cheeky.*

I was starting to rewrite French copy for the designer style guide, a series of Q & As about what to wear for New Year's Eve when he asked me if I ever had sex outside in public. His question was more compelling than the designer's philosophy of style. I minimized the visual of a blond model wearing a luscious leather jacket, short black dress, and sky-high heels leaning against a gleaming BMW.

Me: *Sure.*

Him: *Where?*

Me: *Hmm... Let me think. On a beach, in a forest, in a club bathroom. You?*

Him: *No. Not really.*

I was surprised. He was thirty-seven and he'd never had sex outside?

Him: *How about a garden under the snow?*

I looked out the window. The snow had been steadily falling since the morning. It covered the cars with a thick, glittering, immaculate mantle. Only the center of the street had been cleaned out by a snowplow.

Me: *There's a garden on 6th and B that has a little wooden cabin, like a dollhouse. Do you know it? Just a couple of blocks from your studio. We could sneak into the cabin.*

Him: *You'd sit on my lap. Wear a long dress. And these nylons.*

A link to Bloomingdale's popped up in the chat box. When I clicked on it, the legs of a model appeared, sheathed in black lacy stockings stopping mid-thigh.

I caught my breath. I used to have stockings like that. I had worn them with the blue corset, with Vadik.

Me: *You like that?*

Him: *Yes.*

Me: *I'd wear them, and my big tweed coat and my* chapka *with the fox trim. We would be white with snow.*

Him: *I'd hold you tight and keep you warm. And you wouldn't wear any underwear so that I can make you come with my fingers.*

Me: *Just the stockings.*

Him: *Oui!!!*

The snow was falling thicker and almost horizontal now and started to twirl. My study filled with a milky light. My pants around my crotch were drenched.

The chat box went empty. I left it open, waiting for more words to appear like fumes rising out of the Delphi oracle. But none did.

Two days later, on the way to my writing workshop, I stopped by a little lingerie shop on University Place and, on impulse, bought the same stockings he had shown me.

At his next online visit, he pasted an American Apparel link that showed tights in an array of bright colors. He was leaning toward blue, but I liked yellow better. He seemed to have a remarkable knowledge of women's lingerie. Did he regularly troll the sites of Saks, Bloomingdale's, American Apparel, Barneys? We debated the erotic merits of tights versus mid-thighs. Nylons vs pantyhose. He liked the pantyhose, which could be torn up in the heat of the moment. I sent him a link to the mid-thighs stockings I had just bought. They could either be worn alone or hooked on the garters hanging from my corset. And of course, no panties.

Him: *You bought those?*

In a flash, I realized I had crossed the line from fantasy to reality. Now he knew. These stockings lived in my drawer. They could be worn. I wanted to wear them for him.

I felt foolish. They cost almost forty dollars.

Me: *Yes.*

Him: *Cool.*

We flirted for a while. Our windows remained open for more than an hour, while we each toiled on our respective electronic tasks. Finally, I jumped the gun.

Me: *So when are you going to come and rip up my yellow tights at the crotch?*

Him: *Ha!*

And he vanished into the cyber void.

22

I WAS AT a Xmas book party the following week when my phone buzzed in my purse. Jonah. Just seeing his name gave me a rush of desire.

Me: *Can't meet you. I am at a book party.*

Him: *Meet me afterward? I want to see you all dressed up.*

Me: *Are you in Manhattan? Come pick me up. Or else give me 30 or 45 minutes. Not ready to go yet.*

I waited for the dots signaling that a response was on its way, but nothing came. I talked to a few people. My agent. Other writers. An ex-student. I was distracted, waiting for the whoosh of a new text. When it finally came, I almost jumped, excused myself quickly and went to a quiet corner to pull it out.

Him: *Can't make it.*

My fingers flew over the miniature keyboard. I was so annoyed, the auto-correct was mangling my words to gibberish.

Me: *What? I was about to leave.*

Him: *Sorry. Something came up. It would be too short.* And then, in the next bubble: *wear the dress next time I see you.* Followed by a winking emoji.

I felt the winking emoji pulsing in my gut, flashing a red light. With a sick feeling, I dropped the phone into my purse and went back into the party, but my heart wasn't in it anymore, and I booked a Uber to go home.

23

ALAN WAS COOKING dinner for us again. I could smell it from my office. Garlic, olive oil. The scents of the Mediterranean. It was comforting. He was a great companion, now that Louise had moved out. I enjoyed it while it lasted because he was preparing to go to his Barcelona studio for the winter. I would miss his cooking and his company, but I was also looking forward to getting the apartment back to myself. I did my best writing alone at night, Miles Davis or Coltrane on iTunes, without the temptation of a conversation and a glass of wine.

Tonight was lentil soup with parmesan rind, a handful of cherry tomatoes, and a dash of dried chili pepper. A bottle of Bordeaux was open on the kitchen table.

Any news from *Jazzman*?

Just chatting online. He texted me a couple of days ago, when I was at a book party, but he immediately cancelled. I was furious. I haven't seen him since I told him I recommended him to Lena as a musician to score her next movie.

Alan handed me a glass.

Jazzman freaked out.

He is a good Jewish boy. Maybe he decided to act out all his fantasies with an older woman he can trust before he settles down with an appropriate girl.

There's a gap between what he wants and what he allows himself to do, Alan said. He's postponing the inevitable.

You mean marriage?

Yes.

It's not inevitable. You managed to avoid it all your life.

He cocked his eye at me and poured wine into our glasses.

I pushed my glass away. I had had enough.

A hundred years ago boys would go to brothels for that. We, liberated women of my generation, can provide the same service. For free.

We looked at each other and burst into laughter.

Wow. That was cynical.

But not untrue, no?

Maybe it truly *is* taboo for him, an affair with an older woman?

Yes, but that's exactly why he's turned on by it, Alan said. The problem is that he doesn't own his desire. He's ashamed of it.

Whatever the reason, I said, it takes a lot of finesse and patience for me. He's very skittish. I think of him as a wild cat that is scared to come close to the house, so I put a saucer of milk outside the door, and then I wait until he ventures on his own. If I make the slightest move, he'll run off.

He has to turn up eventually, Alan said. Otherwise, it gets boring.

Boring? I didn't think so.

In *La Nouvelle Héloïse* Rousseau wrote: "As long as we desire, we can do without happiness: we expect to achieve it. If happiness fails to come, hope persists, and the charm of illusion lasts as long as the passion that causes it. So this condition is sufficient in itself, and the anxiety it inflicts is a sort of enjoyment that compensates for reality… We enjoy less what we obtain than what we hope for, and we are happy only before being happy."

Since I had met Jonah, I lived in a state of permanent arousal, of blissful desire, of heightened focus. Colors were brighter, sounds sharper, the sky a piercing blue. The snow glimmered. Walking the streets of the East Village was like stepping into an Edward Hopper painting with its sharp, clean lines and surreal atmosphere. When I met friends, they asked me what made me look so glowing, younger. I walked with my head higher, my shoulders back, I let my hair loose. I even started to get catcalls again, although few and far between, but when I did, I took them as homage, not as offense. I knew I was walking a dangerous edge, but how could I let all that go?

I started writing the novella that night. I wanted to capture that state of desire, of constant expectation. If I never saw him again, I needed to write down what had happened between us so I would remember every moment of it, even if it turned out to be only the shimmering reflections of a dream.

24

WHEN WE BROUGHT back Juliet from Saint Luke's hospital, one hot summer afternoon, broken A/C, ceiling fans whirring full speed, smell of rotting garbage wafting all the way up from five floors below on 110th street, where David still had Columbia housing, I pressed Juliet's diminutive body against my breast, her tiny, voracious mouth already pumping at the nipple. I slumped in the rocking chair (a street find, in white rattan), and a wave of vertigo made me dizzy at the realization that: 1) this tiny bundle in my arms that was barely a day old would die one day. And 2) that I was a mother for life. When David was threatening to leave me, he yelled at me in a fit of rage, to assuage his guilt: you didn't even want to get married, you were not even really committed to me, you were not sure you wanted being a mother, you were terrified of the responsibility, remember? You didn't even tell your mother we had gotten married. We just did it at City Hall, like fugitives. And the *coup de grâce:* Sex is not the only thing that matters.

Even after twenty-two years, I was always unquestionably for David the "lover." At other times I was "the one" or "the woman of my life." Not the "mother." My maternal achievements were dubious at best. I used to say Juliet had two mothers. Secretly, I thought David was the better one.

25

AFTER THE BOOK party, Jonah texted me a few times, but his attempts at turning up were immediately cancelled within minutes or hours by some unforeseen new commitment, or the weather: it was snowing; he was running late; there was a recording session running into the evening; errands to do; a last-minute gig; he had to go back home and work on his music; the flu; he had to fly to California to see his mom; or he was spending the weekend upstate. From my end, it all seemed like a pointless game, as if he was just trying to score an erotic charge without acting on it.

Maybe Alan was right. Maybe he did freak out. Maybe he felt safer spinning sexy scenarios behind his screen than holding me in his arms. But I had a craving for his body, his hands, his hair. Cybersex was dangerously addictive, but it was also so… ethereal.

Without even thinking, I clicked on the site and shuffled through the profiles.

Post-Doc123, 27, *Brooklyn. I love older women. Want to be my fuck buddy?*

Jewish, short beard and dark eyes, a frank smile. Post-doc in biochemistry. I flirt with him. *I take it it's a yes*, he writes. Maybe, maybe not. I am tempted. *We should meet to find out,* I answer, then log off. Post-doc disappears down the cyber-abyss.

Depending on what they look like in their pic or how engaging their opening line is, I answer or not. Mostly not. I *am* the girl in a skimpy dress waiting at the street corner. Alan is right. It's just a meaningless game. A parade of dick pics from some random porn site suddenly marches across my screen as I am about to make a date with *DakotaPrince*, 56, at a nearby café. Without breaking a sweat, I click on the block button, never to hear from him again. It's kind of cool to have that power, like pulverizing your opponent with an *StG 44* in *Call of Duty*. I can do it from my bed, lounging against four pillows, Kiki-the-cat pushing her tiny nose against my wrist.

Genwittstein, 42, *Manhattan. Guitarist.*

A beautiful blond boy with blue eyes floats across my screen. The photo is tilted sideways, so that it looks as though the face is resting on a pillow, in an inviting, almost feminine posture. A discreet nose stud. I click on the picture. Amazing. Another jazz musician, another guitarist. German. Hence his username. A clever play on the philosopher's name.

I message *Genwittstein*. His answer quickly lands in my inbox.

You sound cool too. If you feel like being spontaneous, I have a gig tonight in Brooklyn, and we can have a drink afterwards.

Two minutes later, we were texting on our cells, and he was making a date with me in a bar in Hell's Kitchen that evening. I felt vindicated. I arrived first. He was running late. The subway was stuck on the Manhattan Bridge, and he wanted to drop off his guitar first. It was a Friday night. The bar was packed with what we used to call "yuppies"—a quaint term, in retrospect. Now, the whole city had been turned over to the "bros," except the Lower East Side and North Brooklyn, where the hipsters reigned. I enjoyed the rowdiness of the crowd. Such a relief to have escaped the internet claustrophobia and reentered real life.

I distractedly followed the basketball game playing on the TV screens until he arrived. He was tall, three rings in his left ear, plus the nose stud, short hair, except for a long, dirty blond lock hanging over blue eyes. Very cute. We hit it off, read the same books. We discussed Bolaño, then Murakami. It felt like a date, the kind of date Jonah had denied me. Wouldn't even stoop to take me to a dive bar in Brooklyn. *Genwittstein*, whose real-life name was Frederic, was laid back, too. Maybe it was a musician thing. He also played experimental jazz, and I wondered if he and Jonah knew each other. I savored the added irony of meeting up with a beautiful Aryan man for my secret payback on an elusive Jewish lover. As if either of them cared. But no matter. It was my own secret revenge in the film I was creating. We went for a walk in the neighborhood, then he invited me up to his apartment, where his guitars stood as sentinels against the walls and where we drank warm sake until he leant toward me and kissed me. The whole day had tended to that moment, and I gleefully let it happen. Afterward, I fell asleep listening to his white noise machine. We had sex again in the morning, but it was a little mechanical, and I was getting pretty raw at that point and was eager to leave. We got up and he made me a cappuccino while I watched the dogs and their walkers trace tracks in the fresh snow from thirty floors above.

It had been a good night. Not a passionate night, but a satisfying one. Probably not to be repeated. Which was fine. I walked through the snow to get to the subway station. Christmas lights swung across the streets; people hurried toward midtown stores for last minute shopping. I was outside in Manhattan on a brisk winter morning. The wind was whipping from the Hudson, and I felt a huge weight lift off my shoulders.

I told myself it didn't matter anymore if Jonah contacted me or if I never saw him again. There was Christmas to prepare, the tree to buy and set up, the decorations to hang with Louise, the groceries to order, the final presents to buy. Juliet called to make sure there was a mattress for the foldable playpen that would serve as a crib for Vivian, and not to forget to get whole milk and special Happy Baby fruit and veggie pouches.

26

A WEEK BEFORE Christmas, I logged on the site to read my new messages and the chat box lit up. *Salut!* My heart jolted. It was a snowy Monday morning. Louise was wrapping presents in my study, a few feet away from me. The floor was covered with stacks of boxes and a riot of colored wrapping papers and coils of ribbons.

Would you like a visit?

A visit! After more than a month! He must have sensed I had taken my distance. Men always have a sixth sense about that.

I am busy, I texted back. *Louise is home. We're preparing Christmas.*

But my heart was beating hard.

Juliet and Scott and the baby arrived a few days later, after staying at Scott's parents' upstate. They had dinner plans with David's family in the West Village that night. The plan was for me to babysit Vivian while they went out. We were all having tea, and Vivian repeated her first words in French *chaussures, chaussures,* while furiously stomping around, one of her tiny feet in one of Juliet's boots, her baby curls jumping around in tight ringlets—just like, thirty years earlier, Juliet had done with my shoes at the crack of dawn, stomping so furiously on the wooden floor that our downstairs neighbor used to bang on his ceiling with a broom.

When I checked my email, there was a series of messages on the site and a text from him on my cellphone with the number six followed by a question mark. He had already made an attempt to come by earlier in the week, and but it was so last minute, and it was snowing, making it even more improbable, since it meant a longer commute, cleaning up the windshield, and harder to find a parking spot, that I hadn't quite believed he meant it. I was too ambitious, sorry. Let's try another time. Of course he may have run his life entirely on that energy, always overbooked, always running behind the eight ball. It was almost comical, this stumbling around, this way of living life on the fly, except that he probably showed up on time for a gig or a rehearsal.

So, he had had something canceled and he was free after his job and he could come by at six.

I feverishly tried to assess the situation. Juliet, Scott and Louise had planned to leave at seven for dinner, and I was supposed to put Vivian to sleep at seven thirty—Juliet was strict about bedtimes. So six6 was out of the question.

Him: *So come and see me at the studio.*

Me: *I have to be back home at seven. Too tight. Come here at eight.*

Him: Eight too late.

Me: *Seven thirty?*

Him: *That could work.*

My head was spinning. It was cutting it awfully short. The only way that could work was to put Vivian to bed earlier, which Juliet wasn't keen on, because she would wake up too early in the morning if she went to bed earlier. And what if she woke up in the middle of his visit? And even if Vivian was quiet as a mouse, as she usually was, how could I be relaxed when he came, knowing the baby was asleep in the next room? I felt like a racing car let loose at 200 miles per hour with the brakes shot. I knew it was absurd, dangerous, that I risked exposing myself to him, which was the very thing I dreaded.

I quickly thought up a scenario. If Vivian woke up or made random baby noises, I would say I had friends visiting from Paris and they had asked me to watch their baby while they were out. It was believable, although I had no idea if I could pull it off with a straight face. Also: not very sexy.

I went back to the living area. Juliet had gathered the tea things and prepared the baby's dinner. She was sitting at the kitchen table with Vivian on her lap.

I may have a visit tonight, I said, trying to keep my voice nonchalant, like, no big deal. Juliet, do you mind if I put Vivian to bed a bit earlier, like at seven fifteen?

Who's that? That guitarist you've been seeing?

I felt my cheeks burn like a teenager caught flirting by her parents.

Yes.

You don't care about the baby, Louise said from the other end of the room. What if she cries when you are with that guy?

I'll take care of her.

What's wrong with showing Vivian to him, asked Juliet, pushing a spoonful of mashed spinach and apricot in Vivian's mouth. Why do you have to hide her?

Vivian jerked her head back and forth and the mixture squirted out of her mouth and on Juliet's blouse.

Juliet cursed. Shoot… I was going to wear that for dinner.

It would… hmmm… kind of kill the mood?

Leave your mom alone, Scott said, lifting his head from his laptop. She's entitled to have a gentleman caller.

Louise cried a little, pretend tears. If you're going to hide Vivian, that means you don't love her.

What? What are you? Eight years old?

Do what you have to do, Juliet said, pushing another spoonful into the baby's mouth.

Go clean up your blouse, I told Juliet. I'll finish feeding Vivian.

I sat down with the baby on my lap. Surprised by the change of feeder, Vivian turned quiet and opened her mouth wide.

A text whooshed on my phone. I glanced at it.

Him: *Already back in Brooklyn.*

Me: *What?* I poked the letters with one index finger while holding Vivian with my other hand. *Couldn't you wait?*

Him: *Sorry, I'm back in Brooklyn. Have to play later.*

When Vivian was done eating, I went back to my study. The chat window was still open on my desktop, and I saw he had sent me an IM earlier to cancel. He had a last minute gig.

I was surprised how relieved I felt. I went back to the living room. Vivian's was sitting on her dad's lap while the girls were getting ready.

Never mind, I said. He's not coming after all. He has to play in Brooklyn. I'll put Vivian to sleep at seven thirty.

Are you sad? Louise asked, peering into my face.

I'm good.

They were putting their coats on. Vivian watched them, toddling back and forth, legs wide apart, getting ready to cry as soon as they would open the door. I warmed up her milk in the bottle warmer, picked her up, and gave her the bottle on the couch, while she cuddled against my chest. The smell from her curly locks still had a whiff of honey-sweet, infant hair, the smell I remembered from Juliet and Louise. The most intoxicating scent in the world.

Vivian stopped crying right away and grabbed the bottle with both her tiny hands. I read her a book in French and zipped her up in her swaddle. The old-fashioned swaddle was back in style, signaling the return to a more disciplined and firmer parental style. Once she was lying down in the playpen, Vivian grabbed her pink blankie and stuck a corner of it in her mouth. She didn't peep. Not a cry. Not a stir. Juliet had done an awesome job getting her used to go to sleep without a fuss.

I tiptoed out of the room and breathed a huge sigh of relief. I had dodged a bullet of my own making. What on earth had I been thinking? Was I unconsciously trying to blow the whole thing off? I had a memory of my grandmother putting me to sleep when I was little, with her gray perm, nightgown, and house slippers, while my mother was out, *God knows where, totally irresponsible, as usual,* Mamie whispering between her teeth, as though I couldn't hear her, her breath burning with anger. And I thought maybe I really did want to blow it up.

27

XMAS EVE. THE day of the big dinner party. Friends and friends' lovers and spouses. The girls, and now Scott, and Vivian. The family expanding, not that I had anything to do with it. It was the natural growth, from generation to generation. Life blossoming, forging ahead. Soon it'd be Louise's turn. But not yet. Louise was still waltzing from boyfriend to boyfriend. From breakup to heartbreak. To mad crushes.

I had run to Carroll Gardens, in Brooklyn, to pick up an authentic *bûche de Noël* at a French pastry shop, while Scott went to get the ham at an old Italian butcher shop in the Village, and Alan, who was spending the holidays in New York and would join us for dinner, fetched the champagne. Christmas was the one event that I kept traditional—the lace tablecloths from back home, the crystal, the silver, the blown-glass antique baubles hanging from the tree. The presents, wrapped by Louise, were lavishly piled around the tree in gold and brightly colored paper. I was sweating over the Virginia ham, spreading a chutney glaze over it, while sautéing portobello mushrooms when I heard the whoosh of a text. I craned my neck in the direction of my phone.

Him: *Send me sexy pictures of you.*

I glanced at my ripped jeans and at my hands covered with glaze.

It was six p.m. He was probably alone in his apartment, no festivities to attend since Christmas meant nothing to him. Horny.

I slipped the ham in the warm oven, turned off the gas under the mushrooms, and quickly washed my hands.

Him: *Not naughty.*

That made me laugh. I wasn't angry anymore. He *was* a good Jewish boy.

Me: *Not to worry. Not my style.*

Everything was ready in the kitchen. The wine had been delivered. The champagne was cooling in the fridge. The ham was in the oven. All that was left to do was to warm up the *blinis* when the first guests would arrive, and just add a dollop of sour cream and a thin slice of salmon at the last minute. I had time.

The new stockings lay in a drawer of my dresser, untouched. I had wanted to wear them with him, but this was even better. I ripped up the package and slipped them on. Then I laced up my pair of high-heeled boots and sat on my grandmother's *prie-dieu*—the one she kept in her bedroom and used to kneel on to pray every evening by her bed, but on which I tossed my clothes at night.

Later it occurred to me—raised the perfect Catholic girl, dressed in blue as an infant in honor of the Virgin Mary, mass every Sunday, confession every week, confirmation, first communion, patent leather Mary-Janes and Peter Pan collars—that sending suggestive pictures of myself to a Jew on Christmas Eve at the time when baby Jesus was about to be born, was tantamount to a sacrilege. The kind of sacrilege Catholics have always been fond of, from the Marquis de Sade to Bataille, in a reversal of purity into its opposite.

I was going to leave for a work trip a few days later, to give a reading and teach a series of writing workshops in Boulder, Colorado. There would be a couple of formal events, including New Year's Eve. I tried on a few of the outfits I was thinking of taking with me. A long black dress with a jersey top and a sheer, chiffon skirt, which discreetly revealed the shadows of my legs, and the one made of leopard-print silk that I had worn at Juliet's wedding a year ago, not exactly a "mother-of-the-bride" outfit, but a pretty, sexy dress.

Then I slipped on the corset. I had bought it in Paris after my divorce from David, in my merry window days. I'd gone to Chantal Thomass, the high priestess of French lingerie, and chosen this navy blue number in stretch tulle that subtly molded my chest and waist without constraining nor bulging—tastefully erotic but not trashy. It had cost me an arm and a leg, but it was one of those iconic purchases I felt was necessary to celebrate my newfound sexual freedom. That and a silver snake ring. The ring was long lost. And the corset had been worn only a couple of times with Vadik, because, in the end, he preferred me with nothing on. The blue corset was still in a drawer of my dresser. It was as though it had been waiting for Jonah all these years.

I took snapshots in the mirror wearing the corset, the garters pulling on the nylons and a half-open robe thrown on top. My plan was to send them to him on New Year's Eve as a surprise. The pictures came out blurry. I liked the blurriness for the same reason I liked the pictures without my face. And the way the robe was partially obscuring part of the corset and stockings. I clicked and clicked, deleting the bad shots, getting off on the pure pleasure of offering myself to his desire.

I thought of the snapshots as punk art, the dirty kind of art taken with a cellphone without filter. Dark and grainy, with random bursts of flash going off unexpectedly, blinding my face. As though I had been shot point-blank. The spots and graininess of the pictures, framed by a corner of the antique wood and gold mirror, evoked a turn of the century Parisian bordello. I wanted the pictures to be suggestive but tasteful. Not naughty. The audience was only of one. They were meant to seduce him. As foreplay.

I didn't expect what a turn-on it would be to take the pictures. More erotic than wearing the corset in real life. Especially as I knew what use he would make of them.

I texted him two pictures.

Him: *Love it! Where's your face?*

I had framed the shot from my high-heeled lace-up boots to the top of my thighs, with only a few inches of bare skin showing above the black stockings.

I liked the mystery of it. But I also didn't trust the medium. It's so easy to forward a picture to someone else. So maybe I didn't trust him. Or the nebulous situation we were in. Or how my face would come off with the iPhone camera in natural lightning. I didn't photograph as well as I used to.

I texted him the next day, Xmas day.

Me: *Did you enjoy the pics?*

Him: *Yes!!*

It was almost as good as having had him in my bed that night.

28

HIS MESSAGE POPPED up just as I landed at La Guardia from Boulder, after the New Year, having missed a blizzard in New York by a day.

Are you back? I am alone in the studio. Wanna come see me?

A couple of hours later, Alan stuck his head out the door of his bedroom as I was slipping my coat over the long chiffon skirt I had worn for New Year's Eve and the Russian *chapka* trimmed with red fox that Vadik had offered me in Moscow. His eyebrows went up. He too, like Jonah, was a master of irony, but being older and British, his irony was more burnished. It had a certain kind of warm bonhomie, although I was sure that if you were seriously involved with him, he could probably pierce you mercilessly, and perhaps even lose the irony altogether.

I am going to pay a little visit to *Jazzman*, I said as I rushed out the door.

Alan nodded with a complicit smile.

I flew in the cold streets in my high-heeled boots and my fox hat, a long, woolen scarf trailing down my back, the chiffon skirt floating underneath the unbuttoned tweed coat, running toward the park. The wind was at my back, I felt it whipping the scarf, I leaped over the slush, over the bits of black ice patching the sidewalk, I flew up the block and when I got to the park, I turned south. I texted him at the corner.

Me: *I'm here.*

Him: *Gimme a sec. I come get you.*

Like an apparition from a dream, he emerged in three dimensions, this precious body and flesh I hadn't touched in almost two months. After all that time, he had turned into an icon I regularly looked up online, where a whole bunch of his pictures, taken at one gig or another, lived. We stood almost at the same place where we had first met up, as though he hadn't moved from that street corner below Tompkins Square Park, living there in my imagination when he wasn't taking possession of a corner of my computer. He was suddenly intensely real in a dark parka, week-old beard, and thick snow boots, the winter sun setting over the rooftops behind him. Now the two of us faced each other inside the lobby, both overcome with shyness.

You're so cute, he said, touching the fox trim of my *chapka* with a fingertip, and I said it's my Russian hat, and then we were inside the recording studio stepping over electrical cords and music gear, way into the bowels of the dark building, the air inside electric, hot, pulsing with desire, while he took a phone call and I removed coat, scarf, and sweater and glanced at a huge mirror covering one wall. He stood by me, tallish and dark, in jeans and a grey sweatshirt layered over a T-shirt, in his socks—he had removed his snow boots at the door. For a moment our reflected images in the mirror came together in the dim light like shadows on a wall, not completely there for real, avatars escaped from our cyberworld.

Let's hold each other, he said, and he took me in his arms. And he was skinny in my arms, perfectly calibrated to fit in with my own body. My heart burst open a little, and my head spun like when you are about to have vertigo, and everything takes on a feeling of heightened reality or extra-awareness. A wave of emotion rushed across my chest. I slipped my hand in the opening of his sweatshirt, stroking the softness of his neck, the stubble on his jaw, ran my fingers through his hair. I trembled. I was bursting with tenderness, with a kind of love. A forbidden, impossible love. And then the moment accelerated, and I was sitting on his lap, and he hit iTunes on the computer to drown whatever potential noise we might make. It all became a blur, the lifting of my skirt, the condom, the finish that came too fast for me. I was nervous, he admitted afterward. So was I. And I was touched by his admission, that he was honest about his vulnerability. Perhaps he had never done that before, inviting a woman to his job, which was flattering in a way. But all I really wanted was to hold him in my arms, to kiss his soft, pulpy lips. A desire even more taboo, maybe, for him, even more forbidden.

We got dressed. The connection had been fleeing, trumped by the sex, which had ostensibly been the point but now, in retrospect, had been almost perfunctory.

Let's go have coffee, he said.

I fastened the hat on my head and wrapped the long scarf several times around my neck, pulled on my gloves.

We should get together more often, I said. Why wait so long? You are torturing me and torturing yourself.

He already had his beanie on, low on his forehead, framing his fuzz of a beard, looking so perfectly the part of the archetypal Brooklyn musician, it was almost comical.

I'm a busy boy, he said, his eyebrows going up ironically.

I felt a wave of anger burning my chest.

We walked back up toward the park, to the same coffee place where we had first gone, the one we both agreed made the best coffee in town hands down. Except this time, we stayed inside. He ordered two regular coffees and carried them to the counter. It was summer when we met, we'd already gone through fall, and now it was winter. At first, I was convinced we wouldn't last three months. Then I thought if we made it past the new year, our affair had legs. But he was slipping away from me. The minutes were ticking. It was almost over. The vertigo came back in waves.

We stood at the counter side by side, drinking from our cardboard cups.

You inspire me, I blurted, not sure that's what I really wanted to say.

You inspire me too.

I mean, I've been writing a lot since I met you.

He looked at me sideways. Perhaps it only dawned on him then.

Are you writing about me?

I hesitated.

Yeah. Just trying to make sense of what's going on between us.

He winced at that word "us," or perhaps I imagined it. He just took a step back, pulled his beanie down, and patted his pockets, as if he was about to flee.

I thought of his mix of passivity and abruptness. His ironic smile. Withholding. Slippery. Always a little hesitant, not sure how to take in the space. Sitting at the edge of the couch. Ready to bolt, already ashamed to be there. Even now. His way of running off as soon as we're done, like he's on fire.

We had so little time. He had to go back to work. There was a recording session later, and he had to get everything ready. In those forty-five minutes we spent together, a whole non-relationship had to be framed, stuffed, and rushed, before he got swallowed up behind the graffiti-covered garage door through which he passed to get to the other side of the mirror. My anger surged again, and this time I didn't hold it back.

Look Jonah. What are we doing exactly? What do you want? I'm okay with seeing each other casually. But don't just text me, fuck me, and go silent afterward and disappear for weeks like you never had anything to do with me. You know what I mean?

He put his coffee down, surprised by my outburst.

I'm sorry… Look. I didn't think you…

Had a problem with that? And what is *your* problem? What? Say it!

He turned his face away, as if looking for a quick exit.

I punched him in the arm, gently, trying to soften my outburst.

Listen. I am a big girl. Relax. Don't overthink it. Enjoy it. You don't have to marry me! Do you feel guilty? Is that it? You don't have to feel *that* guilty.

We stared at each other. I had blown up our tacit *entente*, the one I had wordlessly accepted from the beginning.

You're right. I… I don't want it to go too far. I can't give you what you want. I can't be who you want me to be…

I felt my stomach heave as if I was about to throw up. I forced myself to finish my coffee and put the cup back on the counter, harder than I meant to.

He took my wrist.

Eve.

I pulled my wrist out of his hand, wrapped my scarf around my neck, and turned away. As soon as I was outside, I felt the wind lash out at me, and my eyes filled with tears, which is something they often did when it was cold. I did it to myself, I thought, I walked into this knowing full well it could never be more than sex.

29

A FEW DAYS later, I was walking past the garden at the corner of East 6th and B, the one I had described to him in details for our next imaginary *rendez-vous*. It was covered with snow. I took pictures of the house that looked like a dollhouse, of the tower in the middle, of the gazebo, of the bench behind it. I thought of texting him the snapshots. But I didn't. It would be like when I had sent him the link to the thigh-high stockings. Trying too hard.

All he had wanted was to get off on the idea, with one foot online, his thumbs safely texting from his phone. Too much reality would risk waking him up from the dream. Besides, I sensed it was already too late, that our time in real life was up. Like Cinderella turning into a pumpkin at midnight, he had to return to where he had come from, deep into the Brooklyn lands.

And now I was left empty-handed, contemplating the tendril of smoke trailing behind and soon dissolving into the cyber air. He had only been a figment of my imagination. And I, a figment of his.

It had been an affair, as he had said. Yet as soon as he had appeared, a door that had remained locked and fiercely guarded in me since David had left, had been blown open. He had strolled into my life with his carefree nonchalance, his guitar on his back, like a gypsy. He had looked at me almost shyly, leaning against my kitchen counter. He had let me make the first move, let me take his hand and guide him to my bed. He had put himself into my hands.

What can you teach me? he'd asked. I want to learn from you. Tell me, you're the writer. Tell me how we're going to fuck. Tell me how I will take you. Tell me what you want. Tell me what I want. I want to do this. Do you want it? And how about this? I am open, he said. New Yorkers are so guarded. You can't even talk to a strange girl here without risking creeping her out.

As the weeks went on without a message or a text from him, I knew I had been ghosted, or, to put a slightly more positive spin on it, he was seriously MIA. Online dating leads to a whole new vocabulary of acronyms, as though everyone had suddenly leaped into a vaguely menacing military future. The world of millennials and Gen Z is teeming with rules and regulations, labels, and prohibitions. Almost quaint, for someone of my freewheeling generation, which broke all the rules.

And each day that passes without news, a dark, pesky voice swells inside my head. I know that voice. It's not my mother's voice, for sure, my mother who has broken all the rules herself. It's more like a chorus of my grandparents and other well-intentioned, orderly, conservative bourgeois voices. I even detect whiffs of women magazine voices, those temples of conformity despite their pretend taboo-breaking attempts. Or maybe it's the accumulated sediments of standard psychology advice replaying all their favorite hits:

Don't you see where this is going? How predictable. Bad choice, bad choice. Haven't you been there before? You should have nipped this one in the bud. You hesitated, remember, when he first contacted you. You weren't sure it was a good idea. Not sure? Ha-ha. Look at you now! Don't you want to be loved, wanted, chosen, worshipped? Instead of wallowing in that perpetual state of uncertainty, kept in the dark, not knowing the outcome, constantly anticipating, trying to figure out? What are you looking for exactly? At your age?

Oh shut the fuck up! I snap back to my brain. Enough of that conventional bullshit, of these admonishments. I talk back to the voice: Actually, I do like the mystery, the uncertainty. It turns me on.

You'll never be happy, the voice insists with a sad, whiny tone, losing its excited edge, resigned now. Look at how many men you've been with. A failed marriage! David! Why do you think he left you? And Vadik. Innumerable boyfriends, fuckboys, lovers.

Excuse me. Is that what one calls a solid, twenty-two year relationship with two kids. These days, it's considered a long marriage, not a failure. Practically a success. You could call it a relationship that had run its course and ended.

Fine, you had a long marriage. But since then, your record is spotty, wouldn't you say? Only one solid boyfriend. And then you refused to go live with him.

I hear a snorting like my grandmother used to do when she disapproved.

You're going to end up like your mother. Alone. What happened to the sweet little girl you used to be?

And then the voice gathered power to land its final punch.

You'll never have a loving companion to accompany you to your grave.

I try to visualize the "companion" walking me to the grave. Both of us, white-haired and shaking over our canes until one of us keels over. First of all, there will be no grave, I want to be cremated. Second, if it's all about having a roommate, wouldn't a friend play that part just as well? Alan, for instance? Or François, my first French boyfriend, who's still single?

And then I imagine the old couple in *Amour*, how Jonah had been moved by their devotion to each other. *Amour*. I believed in it with David. Did I really give up on love?

The voice takes advantage of my pause to regain vigor, digging deeper, suddenly uncovering another, darker flaw: and all that in secret, behind closed doors, as if he was ashamed of you? You like that shameful secret, don't you? And is the sex even good? The voice screaming at the top of its virtual lungs. These quick, breathless sessions squeezed within an hour like an affair with a married man. Hit and run. No respect.

I put my hands over my ears. Literally. I am in my sunny, airy office, trying to sort out old files from a million years ago, running them through a paper shredder I bought at Staples, because you're supposed to shred all your old financial data. I have a sorry tendency to let things accumulate, not out of a hoarding mentality, but because who knows what to do with the past? Discard it? Keep it? Where does one stand regarding the past and the future? Always on the edge of one and of the other.

And then, when I can't stand the accumulation anymore, I suddenly dump everything in a fit of frustration. Throw or give everything away. The files flow out of my hands into the shredder and end up in bulging plastic bags headed for recycling. To shut up the voice once and for all, I click on a YouTube clip of one of John Zorn's *Masada* live concerts and turn up the volume to the max to drown out the voice, dissolve my doubts. I maximize the screen and watch the band furiously improvising, playing off one another, in a sublime crescendo, the melody picking up again and again, and gathering to an irresistible, ecstatic drumbeat.

30

I TOOK LOUISE to brunch in one of the new places in Bushwick. In contrast to Alphabet City where older and younger residents, Anglos and Latinos, whites and blacks, all generations combined and mixed in the street, Bushwick is strictly after-college crowd. The minute I walked into the café behind Louise, the label "mom" was tattooed on my forehead. I noticed a few other moms and dads parked in a corner table, boomer couples, and shuddered.

You look upset, *maman*, Louise said.

I shook my head and tried a semi-smile. Louise could read my face like no one else. It made me feel vulnerable and guilty. Louise wanted a happy mom, a mom with husband and money, or at the very least a safe and solid mom. Or, alternatively, a bestselling writer mom. I thought Louise hated my vulnerability because she felt vulnerable herself. Louise, the prime witness of my ups and downs, of my private failures and losses, even if I didn't talk about them. Everything must have been crystalline to her, the two of us mysteriously attached by invisible fibers as she was growing up.

I dived into my *huevos rancheros*, eyes lowered.

I'm fine.

I hate when you pretend everything's okay. Louise said sternly. Is it that guy you're seeing? The guitarist?

I cursed myself to have even mentioned him, that time, at Xmas.

Yea. It's over, I think.

But you were never a couple, right?

A couple? No… No. We saw each other on and off, in a kind of loose way.

He's too young, mom! And I don't think he's been treating you well.

She was right, of course. She could pick up on my evasiveness and expose it. I thought of Jonah's fear that his brother would find out about us. We were both caught in the same secret, up against society's disapproval.

I know, I said. You're right.

A wave of sadness crashed over me. The sadness I had not been able to feel when Vadik had vanished in Africa, after I had pushed him away. The sadness that I had kept locked into the subterranean regions of my heart after David had left. It had suddenly been reignited.

You crying? Mom!

Louise stretched her hand and patted mine. She looked worried.

I'm fine, *ma chérie.*

After Vadik, I had remained single for several years, with a few flings along the way. I was surprised to discover I liked being on my own. It was bracing to learn to navigate life without the support of a man. It was like growing muscles I didn't even know existed. What happened with Jonah was like a brush fire bursting out of smoldering embers that had been dormant for years.

Louise looked skeptical.

I don't believe you. You look lonely.

Now the blade of a tiny pocket knife was thrust into my wrist, not deep enough to pierce the vein, but bruising enough to reopen that wound, the lack in my soul that Jonah had briefly filled. Louise, with her flawless intuition, had found it and pressed on it.

You'd like me to be married, is that it? That would reassure you?

Louise shrugged. Not necessarily *married.* But… yeah.

The room we were in, carved into the basement of an old building, was full of twenty-something brunchers who had taken over Bushwick, where kids crowded in small apartments or lofts in order to be able to afford the ridiculous rents until they could make enough money to start their adult lives. Even Jonah felt displaced by the new generation and rejected the notion of "hipster" for himself. And yet, I felt more at ease there than in grown-up Manhattan. I loved to be surrounded by young people.

Let's go, I said, signing the bill and pocketing my bankcard.

Outside, the January wind lashed at us. We pushed our beanies down to our eyes. Louise walked ahead, a graceful, lithe beauty, her hair spilling out of her woolen hat in thick, dark waves. We walked in that awkward silence when too many unsaid things hang in the air, too knotted to be teased out. After a quick peck, Louise disappeared into her building down the block. I continued to the subway, stumbling over the rough cement slabs of the treacherous sidewalk, their uneven joints covered by black ice. The mouth of the train station opened straight out of the wall, guarded by stalactites hanging like teeth. Patches of frozen water or pee dotted the stairs. Brooklyn still looked like the East Village used to look like in the 80s. Run down, dilapidated.

31

PORSCHE911, 27 – I love French women ☺

Sunshine, 54 – Hi, young and beautiful

Hey, I'm Jason. You're beautiful. Are you a banana? Because you are so A-peeling.

Hi, I'm Alex!

Hi, I'm John. Bonjour pretty lady.

Married? Just curious.

Married lawyer. But not the sleazy type.

Ha-ha. Seriously?

The married, non-sleazy lawyer sent me his picture to one of my old email addresses. He looked lawyerly. Suit and tie.

Married lawyer messaged me again, with a preemptive condition. *Only thing you may not be is very curvy.*

You're in luck, I'm not, I replied. *But I'm not interested in a married lawyer.*

Wait!! Even for a scotch?

32

I WAS CAREFULLY studying the line-up of musicians booked for the upcoming New York Jazz Festival. *Genwittstein*, A.K.A. Frederic, the German I had hooked up with before Xmas, was playing, and so was Jonah, in different venues and at different times. They *had* to know each other. How large could the experimental jazz scene be in the city? I got a kick out of it, that they might have run into each other at the recording studio, or even played in the same band. I attended Frederic's concert with Lena. I had no claim on him, our night now fading into the mild memory of a one-night stand. We slogged through the snow across town toward the West Village, to a basement theater that was full and brilliantly lit. It was a big band, with a large horn section, and the crowd was buzzing. Frederic played a solo on acoustic guitar and was enthusiastically applauded. At least I had had two talented guitarists as lovers. Although what did it matter? Jonah's show was the following afternoon in a small room at Lincoln Center, but I couldn't take the risk of him seeing me. Going to Frederic's show had been a good substitute, a pinch of spice to make up for Jonah's disappearance.

When I went back home, I sat down at my laptop and wrote late into the night, and immediately afterward felt calmer. The vise grip of my desire loosened.

33

THE WRITING GROUP met at the various apartments of its members, at least those members who deemed their apartment worthy of receiving visitors. And usually in Brooklyn since I was the only one living in Manhattan. I had never joined a writing group before. French writers make a point of not studying writing. Writing is supposed to ensue from secretly toiling away in solitude and voracious reading, like a gift from the gods.

I had met Mike, the writer who invited me to join the group, at a reading a couple of years ago. We had had a drink together afterward. He was divorcing, I couldn't tell whether it was a potential date or a friendly drink between colleagues. He was up and coming, he had had a story published in *The New Yorker.* I had been flattered to be asked to join the group, but at the time, I didn't have anything ready to show. When I started the novella that winter of Jonah's disappearance, I decided to join. I wanted to test the new piece. It would give me a deadline, the excitement of showing my work, the support I was craving since my latest book had been published six years before.

The night we discussed my pages, we met in East Williamsburg, in one of these old manufacturing warehouses converted by Hasidim into lofts. I had gone to these warehouses ten years ago after my divorce, when Williamsburg was all abandoned industrial spaces taken over by artists who had turned them into rough studios with cold water and a hot plate. Parties went on all night—raves fueled by MDMA.

I remembered one Fourth of July, hundreds of bodies pressed on a huge roof with a postcard view of Manhattan at sunset. It was a miracle the roof didn't cave in. Anyway, the new lofts were all roughly cleaned up now, although the staircases leading up to them were still as grimy and rickety as ever. Of course, that far east on the L, the rents were a little more affordable. The meeting was taking place at the divorcing (now divorced) writer. Mike. The one whose short story had been published in *The New Yorker.* He had just moved in.

My heart was racing when we sat down to a spread of cheese and crackers and IPA beer bottles. There were six of us that night: Mike, who had invited me, Tom, a gay guy I had met at a writer's residency, another gay guy I didn't know, and two young women I had only met at the previous session. I had sent them about fifty pages of my novella.

The first one to speak up was Mike. He raved at first. Maybe "rave" isn't the word. But still it was glowing. About breaking boundaries, the sexuality of an older woman and a younger man. *There was a lot to love* about the piece. They all spoke in turn. We need to know the woman's age right away, or soon enough, said one of the women. Otherwise, we miss the impact. It's great at the beginning, but then it gets repetitive, said Tom. But that's when she becomes obsessed, cut in Mike. You can see she's going into a negative spiral. That's what's interesting. Makes me think of Haneke's *The Piano Teacher.*

I listened, outwardly cool, heart twisted in a knot inside. Haneke kept coming into my life. *Amour, The Piano Teacher.* Certainly, it was flattering. But on second thought, maybe not. All these stories of women, from *Anna Karenina* to *The Piano Teacher,* were told by men. They demonized flawed, fallen women. Why would I want to emulate them?

Suicidal, Mike went on. She's a total narcissist, interjected gay guy #2, the one I didn't know. He was about forty, blond with a grey soul patch and one green eye and one hazel, which I couldn't help staring at. What young guy would possibly desire her? He went on. She's too old. Maybe if he knew her as a writer and admired her and was obsessed with her. Or if she was an editor, and he was a writer and hoped that she would publish him. Otherwise, no. Doesn't make sense. He would be repulsed by her.

I felt my cheeks and chest burning, my heart walloping. They could certainly read through my veiled attempts at fiction.

The main problem they all had was the woman's age. Why doesn't she go out with a man her age? She's immature. Plus, they couldn't fathom that anyone could desire a sixty-two-year-old woman. Soul patch liked the part where she imagined a voice berating her for her life choices and encouraging her to find peace and happiness with a man her own age. *A companion to march to the grave together.* He loved that line.

Perhaps there was something positive in the writing if they were engaged to the point of ripping my characters apart and taking sides. At least it wasn't boring. The guitarist wasn't spared either. He's a jerk. Just playing with her. Doesn't she see it?

I was about to faint. Didn't they see how nervous the guitarist was? How conflicted? Guilty. Ashamed. Clearly, my writing hadn't captured his complexity. I tried to focus on the snacks. A big slab of sharp cheddar and crisp crackers, and little bowls of Greek olives and Wasabi peas were geometrically arranged around a platter of vegetables. I studied the label of my beer bottle. Raging Bitch. Image of a wild dog showing her teeth. It made me think of the wolves I had dreamt of when I had first met Jonah. Very hoppy taste. And fruity, too. I swallowed a handful of Wasabi peas and almost choked.

They were reading the pages on their tablets, except soul patch who had a print-out. I think you're too harsh, Tom, gay guy #1 said, the one I had met before. Why wouldn't she want to sleep with a younger man?

I knew Tom liked younger men. He had shown me pictures of pretty boys he dated on Grindr.

He doesn't want her, soul patch insisted. Don't you see? He's playing her. It's like these young gay guys who fool around with old men. They like to tease them, turn them on. It makes them feel powerful. But they're repulsed by them.

His own novel was about a teenage boy being groomed by an older man who eventually abuses him. We had discussed it the previous time. Was he projecting? I was sitting on a low couch clutching my knees. He was sitting on a chair across from me, holding the high ground.

It was like facing the Inquisition or the firing squad and not being allowed to plead in your favor, because the rule in these torture sessions is that you never defend your work. I popped open another bottle of Raging Bitch.

At first the girls were mute. They were much younger than me, in their thirties, I guessed. One was married, the other one had a boyfriend, and they may have secretly thought it was impossible to desire an older woman. Or maybe they were hoping against hope that they would still be desirable at sixty. Or maybe they were shocked.

I glanced up and saw that one of them, Annie, the one with the boyfriend, was clutching her tablet and leaning forward. She was a luminous girl with green eyes, her hair in short dreadlocks that spiked around her head. Her short story had been hotly debated a few weeks earlier, and I had defended it.

I think Eve is very brave, she said with a soft voice. She knows she's defying American societal conventions, but she's going for it anyway. It doesn't matter whether the affair will last or not. What matters is that she's taking the risk. That makes her a compelling character.

Soul patch stared at her, ready to argue, but the other woman, Jessica, who sported a messy topknot and square glasses, jumped into the fray. Her angle was different. Jonah's like one of these guys you see everywhere in Brooklyn, she said. Perfectly captured. Very tight story. Economic use of details. Good sexual tension.

They were more generous than the guys. But their voices were already being drowned out. I cracked open a third Raging Bitch. I knew it would undo me—one glass of wine usually does me in—but I needed to do something to take the edge off. At least it was better than the Heineken I had offered Jonah, that was *so 80's*. Haneke. Heineken. What did that mean? Was it a sign? My mind whirled around in a kind of stupor. I was getting drunk.

I hear you, butted in Tom, turning to Annie, but I think a negative spiral *a la The Piano Teacher* would be compelling.

I felt betrayed. Now Tom was turning against me?

Regardless of the ending, you're right, the stakes have to be higher, chimed in Jessica. She's so cool. But that's also what I like about her. She keeps her cool.

Too cool? Annie asked.

Maybe she meets a man her age and she drops the young guy, suggested Mike.

Look at her, soul patch said. She's going back for more. Hasn't she learned her lesson? She doesn't evolve as a character. Keeps repeating the same thing. Running in circles. Not growing at all.

Also, how about Alan? How does she feel that he's having a love story with the dancer but hers doesn't go anywhere? Wouldn't she be jealous?

As he hit the sheets of paper against the edge of the coffee table a couple of times to make his point, a tattoo of an anchor on his biceps popped out from under his rolled-up shirt sleeve. He was reading that line again. *A companion to march to the grave together.*

That's the heart of your character, right there, that voice of reason. She needs to grow up. Face her age. Face the fact that she's got grandchildren, and let it go. Or else she could head straight to self-destruction. Suicide. Throw herself out of the window. Dramatically it might be more interesting. Because it might be the last love of her life. The last man she sleeps with.

Don't you think it's a cliché, I said in a weak voice, breaking the cone of silence I was supposed to stay in, if she commits suicide? She's not depressed.

There was an explosion of sun through the wall of windows of the loft. The light, liquid copper as if filtered through a stained glass window in a medieval church. I stared at it. The Raging Bitch was bitching inside of me.

Why do you want to punish her, I went on, more firmly.

What else? You want a happy ending? That was soul patch again, his voice dripping with sarcasm and incredulity. With the guitarist?

No, no, I retreated hastily. Of course not. God, no. But suicide or death means women being punished for defying society's rules. Like *Anna Karenina* or *Madame Bovary*. That's exactly what I don't want. We don't live in the nineteenth century anymore.

She's deluded, soul patch insisted. Pure fantasy. Not even believable.

I couldn't take it anymore. Maybe it was the Raging Bitch giving me courage. I stood up suddenly and faced him. My heart was about to explode in my chest.

You have no clue what you are talking about, I said, no clue about women.

I packed up my laptop in a hurry, trying hard to focus on picking up all my things.

Eve! Wait! Tom said.

I grabbed my coat without bothering to slip in the sleeves. When I got to the front door, which was at the other end of the loft, I heard Annie say: You're crossing a line. It was a personal attack.

I was drunk, disoriented, my head swimming. I couldn't remember where the subway station was. I stumbled down the street, wondering where in Williamsburg I could find a good spot to throw myself into incoming traffic, or under the wheels of the L train. Before I could find either, I dropped my bag on the sidewalk and threw up.

They emailed me their comments in track changes that evening, except soul-patch, more old school, who had written his in a separate file.

Trembling I forced myself to read his notes the next day. *Narcissistic, immature, in denial. Repulsive.* The lines danced in front of my eyes. Every one of his words jackhammered into me.

I printed his notes and took the piece of paper to the kitchen and lit it with a match in the sink, watch it burn until it was wet ashes.

34

A FEW DAYS after the writing group session, I got an email from Annie, the young woman with the spiky dreads.

I am so sorry about what happened the other night. It was disgusting, the way the boys were ganging up on you, although Mike defended you after you left, if that makes any difference. I really liked your story a lot. I hope that it was clear that I loved it. But I am not sure what I said registered. I just wanted to tell you directly. I think Eve's very brave. A lot of women wouldn't dare do what she's doing. It takes a lot of self-confidence. She's cool. I want to be like her when I am older.

I was so grateful for her warmth and support I felt tears come up to my eyes. I invited her over for coffee the next weekend.

Thanks for your email, I said. I really appreciated it. You have no idea.

I'm sorry it was rough going.

It was brutal. I was shaken up. I am not as cool as Eve.

She laughed. Really? I saw a lot of Eve in you.

Maybe it's a façade, I said.

I'm going to drop out. I don't think the group is helping me.

I poured the coffee and handed her a cup.

We can read each other's work, I suggested.

So that's the secret to looking young, she said, pointing to my ripped jeans and old band T-shirt.

Oh God! I don't think of it as dressing young. I've always dressed more or less like this. I think when people dress "old" or "their age" they take on a role. It's performative, like gender, you know? They feel social pressure to act that way. Anyway, it's question of attitude. It's the energy, the vibrancy that matters. Or does that sound too woo-woo?

She laughed.

A little. But you make me feel hopeful about growing older. That there's something to look forward to. We always think… especially women, that we'll lose everything as we get older. Like, I am thirty-nine, and I don't have kids. And I'm afraid it's already too late. When I think of my mom…

That's bullshit, I said. It's patriarchal society dictating what we can do or not do. I made ironic air quotes around "patriarchal society." You can still have kids. I had my daughter Louise at forty. But it's not always easy to go against the rules. There's a price to pay. But that's what we are trying to change, isn't?

At a reading at McNally Jackson bookstore a few days later, I heard a woman talk behind me during the break. She's *mutton dressed as lamb*, the woman was saying, about someone she knew. It's sad.

I turned my head slightly. Two women about my age, not unattractive, perhaps university professors like I was, but the one who was talking looked like she had given up on seduction or even on being vibrant and had comfortably settled on a complacent late middle-age life. I remembered a picture I had seen online of a brilliant British painter in her eighties, who'd recently had a huge retrospective, wearing a miniskirt over woolen tights and high-top Vans in her studio. Totally grunge. She looked adorable. Women are the most judgmental, I thought. They throw each other under the bus.

35

WHEN I HAD finally got up the courage to ask David to leave, every last drop of pride swallowed and all hope crushed, Juliet stood in the bathroom, staring me down, and from the confidence of her fifteen years, lashed out at me: you didn't even know how to keep him.

A couple of months before that, before the dinner party when he solemnly announced to whomever was listening that *he had to follow his heart*, David had taken me to a new bar in the quickly gentrifying Alphabet City—on the same block where, years later, I would have coffee with Jonah—and, his hand on my knee, his fedora at a jaunty angle on his head, told me: you are the woman of my life. I never had a boring day with you.

Maybe it was true, even as he already loved another woman, or it had been true. Maybe he was taking stock of our years together. Maybe it was a declaration that sounded good to him, a grand, cheesy declaration of the kind he used to make in the early days, like *you and I make beautiful music together*. Maybe he was trying to convince himself. I had let myself been briefly reassured, so desperate was I to believe *we* were still possible, and that the sinking ship could still be righted.

And then, just two or three weeks later, after dropping Louise off for a playdate in Central Park, I had aimlessly wandered to the west side. It was a beautiful September afternoon, the sky was of that pure, brilliant blue like the day the planes shot like missiles into the Twin Towers and exploded the world. It was not a neighborhood I usually went to. I am a true downtown girl, rarely venture north of 14th Street, unless it's for a business meeting midtown or to take the train at one of the stations.

Perhaps for that reason they had taken no precaution. They were freely walking hand in hand, a new couple in love, David and that blond girl in the middle of the late summer crowd on a Saturday afternoon, in spite of all the care they must have taken for months to avoid running into me. But who would have thought I would be hanging out in the Upper West Side on a weekend? Not even *I* had planned it. I glimpsed them sideways, at the corner of Columbus, I was walking west on 72nd and they were about to cross so there was no way to avoid them.

They were caught like pigeons in the crosshairs, and David was closer to me. It was him at his best, jeans slung low, faded T-shirt, his hair buzzed on the sides the way he was wearing it back then, and the girl was slight and tall, with flowing blond hair loosely braided on one side and a flowery dress and flat sandals. Flower girl. But these are thoughts that came to me afterward, a collage of images reconstituted after the fact. At that moment it was a frontal stab through my stomach. The thing is, there was nowhere to hide. The encounter happened. We were face to face. A veil had suddenly been torn up, the curtain pulled to the side, and the show was starting. The three of us stood at the corner, paralyzed, like blown together by a hard gust of wind. I noticed he had dropped the girl's hand.

Hi, I said.

Hi, this is MaryAnn, David said.

Hi, I said again.

Nobody made any move. I nodded hello or goodbye. The red hand on the streetlight pulsed and the numbers started going down, signaling the seconds left before the light turned red, before our world ended forever, the avenue was wide, I threw myself across Columbus like diving from a high rock into a shallow bottom pursued by a horde of rabid dogs.

36

IT WAS LATE March now. I had stopped writing Jonah's novella after the writing group fiasco, focusing only on my translations and my teaching. The writing group was right. It was foolish to cling to the hope that it wasn't over, just as I had foolishly clung to David hoping things would turn around even after I knew he was having an affair. And yet I couldn't let go of Jonah. I wanted to ride the passion till it burnt out instead of this exhaustive dance of on/off, his constant running away. I couldn't accept that he was gone for good. The attraction we felt for each other deserved to be lived all the way, conventions be damned. If I was patient enough, he might finally allow himself to have that *affair* he secretly wanted.

On afternoons when he worked at the recording studio, I checked his website and his Facebook page and stared at his pictures online, as though I could force him out of hiding if I followed him long and hard enough. People had a half-life online that lingered and lingered, and you could almost believe that they were there, close to you, in your own life, even if you never saw them. The border between virtual life and reality was getting blurrier and blurrier. Maybe I wasn't as far gone as in *The Piano Teacher*, but my obsession became all-consuming.

I started to go to Brooklyn to listen to experimental jazz and new music. At the *Sorbonne*, I used to hang out with a group of friends who spent their weekend listening to Miles and Coltrane, Bud Powell and Herbie Hancock, Keith Jarrett, Oscar Peterson, Gerry Mulligan, and Bill Evans. I could still hear the suave voice of the French FM radio announcer presenting rare or bootlegged takes of live sets. But David was a rock 'n' roll guy, and I had put jazz aside.

It was easy to figure out where the good places were, who were the best bands, the best musicians. I went alone, excited to discover the new sounds, the backrooms of dive bars, of restaurants. I slipped in, got a beer if it was a bar or paid my fifteen or twenty dollars and sat on a folding chair on the side, letting myself be swept up by the energy, the power of the improvisation. One night, in a rough space off Gowanus, a young trumpet player wearing a backward baseball cap made her horn magically sound like an underwater whale and jungle birds' songs. I left in a fog of desire and despair, realizing I could dip into that world as much as I wanted, but Jonah himself was ever more out of my reach.

37

AROUND THAT TIME, I met Sarah. My students had invited me to a wrap party at a film professor's apartment. I found myself in the kitchen next to a woman who was pouring bubbly into everyone's glasses. The conversation was about movies, about Judd Burstein's latest, which I had just seen. The woman pouring champagne, who also taught at the university, said she had grown up with Judd and his little brother Jonah. I went to the same high school as Judd, she said. I had a crush on him way back. He's so cool. We're still good friends.

I've met his brother, I blurted.

Really? I remember him as a loner, always with a book or his guitar. What is he like now?

We took our glasses to the living room and found a couch to sit on. It was clear that Sarah—with her jet-black hair and Doc Martens—still had a crush on Judd, despite his being married with two kids. She seemed as eager to talk as I was to listen.

He often mentions his brother, she said. He's always worried about him. He says girls like him, but he has trouble settling down.

I'm not surprised. He's very cute, I said cautiously.

How do you know him?

Just... Music world.

Judd is kind of a father figure for him. They were raised by their mom, the father left when they were young, I think Jonah was like five. Judd and I both went to UCLA. And Jonah got into music. They are all musicians in the family. The father plays piano. They would all gather in the evenings and play. I worshipped them. I remember wishing I had a family like that. Jonah was super introverted. The quiet little brother. Gifted but really shy. He went to Berklee. After that, he ended up in New York.

I was soaking up her every word.

Something happened to him, Sarah continued. I don't know if he was about to get married or engaged and the girl left him, or if he actually got married and they broke up soon after. She wasn't Jewish, maybe that was part of the problem. The father is super traditional. Not exactly orthodox, but kosher, all that. I know. I come from that kind of family. According to Judd, the father's kind of an asshole. It's weird because Judd's wife isn't Jewish. But Judd gets away with everything. He's taken his distance.

Jonah married? That was hard to imagine. Maybe a serious breakup.

He's a bit adrift, I guess, she continued. Just the opposite of Judd, who's so charismatic, so together.

38

ALAN LEFT TO go to Barcelona. He was applying for an artist's visa and had to stay in Europe until he got it. Without him and Louise, the apartment felt empty, I had lost my anchors. I took to walking around naked from room to room if I felt like it. Talking out loud to myself. Talking to Kiki-the-cat who responded by jumping on my desk and rubbing her face against my laptop or stepping on the keyboard to stop me from working. The city was white, then gray, with the occasional burst of brilliant sunlight. When I went out, regardless of where I was going, I carefully avoided walking past Jonah's recording studio, even if it meant taking the long way around. I stopped logging on the dating site, except in brief spurts, to read and answer messages. I waited until I had ten or twenty to check them out. Every time a new notification popped up, the number would climb up in the corner of the app icon. I liked to see the number go up, as if I was accumulating food cans in the pantry in case of famine.

At the end of February, I caught a bad cold and spent three weeks filling up my wastebasket with used tissues. At the beginning, mucus poured endlessly out of my nose and throat, but then I started to cry. I was emptying myself out, liquefying. A block of ice inside me was thawing. I hadn't cried like this since I found out David was having an affair, when I wandered the streets hysterically, clutching tissues and hugging the walls in shame.

I made four pots of tea a day and rewrote French copy for the American designer website. I pondered the difference between organza and tussor, twill and crepe, poplin and broadcloth, alligator and crocodile, Mikado and dupioni, nappa and vachetta, and explored the myriad of syntaxic variations to vaunt the merits of the new styles while giving the impression of saying something different and new every time. I pored over websites devoted to the minutiae of tailoring, the subtle variations of lapels on a man's jacket, the different collars on a shirt. On bad days, I hallucinated haikus.

In early April, within a couple of days, Jonah's picture popped twice among the visitors to my profile with no message—tiny buds pushing on the wintry trees with an imperceptible green fuzz. Tilt your head at a slight angle, and there's nothing to see. What was going on there? Was it a silent hello? A ripple of desire, quickly squashed?

I ignored it.

39

I WAS COMING back from a coffee date with a Wall Street lawyer who lived in Westchester, an inconceivably long distance from the East Village. It was a new attempt to meet someone I could technically have a relationship with. He was a bit younger than me, divorced with two teenagers, smart, but very buttoned-up, the furthest from the kind of men I was attracted to. He had studied French lit at Yale and was an avid reader of George Pérec, as I was, which got me excited for a while, but after we planned to meet for dinner the following week, I found an excuse to leave immediately after our date. This time I walked straight through the park and made the turn on Avenue B and found myself smack across from Jonah's recording studio. I was about to cross the street when I noticed someone waving at me. A guy on the phone, a cup of coffee in his hand. From a distance, with my bad eyesight, I couldn't tell who it was. It was him. He hung up and waved at me.

You were not going to come and say hello?

Hello. How have you been?

Busy. Too busy.

He looked tired, actually. His hair was a little longer, his beard a little shorter. He shaved once a week, so depending on the day of the week it was either a barely there stubble or longer and bushy. Never the same man two days in a row.

Trying to put together an album. I'm writing songs for it, lots of rehearsals—yeah… Wish I had more time. But I am lucky I have this job.

Here, you mean?

Yeah.

The vibe was still there. I could feel our bodies leaning hard toward each other.

I've been thinking about you, he said.

Me too.

About me in your bed?

Oooh... Cocky! You're the one who disappeared, I should remind you.

I know, but... He stammered... we can't really... we can't really...

He couldn't even say the word. Whatever word that was. This cool experimental jazz musician, with his beard and his swag, carrying his guitar on his back like a gypsy, playing atonal noise music in dive bars, living off recordings, giving guitar lessons, and the paltry sums he made as a sideman for hire and at the recording studio, not exactly a conventional life, that dude was tied up in knots about what people might say if they knew he slept with a woman who was more than twenty years older!

His whole body, usually so laid back, became taut, an arc simultaneously moving toward and pushing away from me. We were standing face-to-face by the graffitied door, the desire was so strong, take me right against that door, pull out your cock and fuck me right now. I had the image of him on my bed, his brown skin, almost Middle Eastern, his sex still humid, curling on top of his thigh after sex. His smell, a touch musky.

I should go back to work, he said, although he made no move to enter the studio.

Okay, I said. Bye! I turned away with a little wave of my hand. Cool as a cucumber. (The writing group was right—I was too cool. Need to work on that.) Not turning back. I could go now. I knew what I wanted to know.

40

A FEW WEEKS later, I played hooky and went to see a science fiction flick in the afternoon. It was about a tech guy working in Silicon Valley who falls in love with a virtual girl. Of course, he could never hold her in his arms. She was just a voice. They could only talk or send messages. Not being able to touch her was driving him insane. At his insistence, she sent a human surrogate to make love with him. A flesh and bone woman he could hold in his arms. The woman was pretty, but she wasn't *her*. She wasn't the one with the enticing voice, the one he had imagined. The movie was about the power of the dream over the power of the flesh. The virtual girl ended up breaking it off and turning into a million stars, fulfilling her destiny. He was heartbroken.

I walked back from the movie theater through the park, thinking the story was not really different from what had happened with Jonah. A virtual romance. And just as I passed the dog run where I had first met him more than six months ago, there he was, in the flesh, sitting on a bench with an acoustic guitar on his knees, a flop of dark hair falling over his eyes. I stood in front of him without saying a word, and he looked up and smiled as if he had been expecting me.

What are you doing?

Putting new strings on a guitar. I didn't have the time to do it this morning. I am giving a lesson tonight.

Do you mind if I sit?

The tension was electric. My whole body was drenched with desire. His beard was longer and it was sprinkled with white. I watched him tighten the string with a tuning peg and twist the end in a bow. I touched the loose end with the tip of my index finger.

You leave it like that?

I'll cut them when I get home.

He pulled another string from a coil on the bench next to him and ran it from the neck to the bridge and tightened it.

I like to watch you do that.

He smiled at me under his thick bangs.

I like you to watch me.

Then he went on restringing the guitar. He may be a tease, act like a jerk, I thought, but underneath he's not sure of what he's doing. He may have talent and looks, but something's missing, like an engine that's going too fast, that he doesn't have under control. I remembered what Judd Burnstein's friend, Sarah, had said about him.

He asked me about Louise, about my writing. I lied and said all was going well. But I didn't really know what I was saying. The more I felt troubled by my emotions, the more I played it cool. Maybe we were similar in that respect. He said he had a couple more students, which was a relief, because they paid $100 an hour for each lesson, and three students a week made a huge difference since he only worked part-time at the studio. Then he asked me about the dating site. I said I was sick of it.

Of the boys?

Yeah…. And you?

The girls? Yea, me too…

He slipped the guitar in its case, zipped it, and we got up.

He had to pick up something in a store on the other side of the park and then drive back to Brooklyn to give the guitar lesson. I was going home in the opposite direction.

We should get together, he said, have a play date.

The next Monday there was a message from him.

Him: *Hey you. I have been thinking naughty thoughts about you since last week.*

It was the first day of Passover. The band over the chat box flashed hot pink.

Me: *Shouldn't you be thinking of gefilte fish and bitter herbs?*

Him: *Perhaps. I am going to a Seder tonight. But I have something else in mind. I am thinking of breaking some biblical laws with you.*

Me: *Everything we do is about breaking laws. Biblical, Catholic, secular laws. Age. That's what makes it so desirable.*

He messaged me again around five.

Him: *I am alone in the studio. They all left. Will you come see me?*

He had prepared the scene: a high stool in front of the big mirror. The idea was that I would kneel on it and he would rip my pantyhose. It was a crackpot idea as the stool was too small for the maneuver. After several, unsuccessful attempts, I almost fell down in waves of laughter.

I don't think today is the day we're breaking biblical laws. It was a bold plan, but not happening.

Let me get a pair of scissors to rip your pantyhose.

No scissors. Do it with your teeth!

We were laughing so hard he couldn't get a good handle on the nylon. He ended up ripping it up with his fingers.

How old are we, I said afterward. Twelve?

Just about. We're the same mental age.

We walked out into the blazing sun. It didn't matter what had happened before and what would happen afterward. I forgot all about my age, all about my life. I understood men's *demon de midi*—the noon demon, what we call in French men's midlife crisis—how a younger woman gives them back their youth in those fleeting moments of recklessness. I was doing the same.

You're so much fun, I said.

He took me by the shoulders and squeezed me against him.

You too!

He was the boy I would have loved at fifteen or sixteen. My first love. Our ages were all wrong. Not because we were lopsided, but because we were way too late.

My first crush was a neighbor on the Côte d'Azur where my grandparents had a summerhouse. I was twelve. He was sixteen, from Corsica. On a late afternoon in a little cove between two *calanques*, he handed me his cigarette, my first. We sat side-by-side on a rock overlooking the sea, passing the cigarette back and forth. A few days earlier, at a dancing club on the beach, while Françoise Hardy's "Tous les garçons et les filles" was playing, he took me by the hand, and we danced. We ended up doing nothing more than that, but the spark smoldered for years. Every summer when we ran into each other at the beach, I felt it. All year long I thought of him.

Four summers later, I saw him flirting with a pretty brunette wearing a tiny plaid bikini at the café on the promenade, and they were engaged by the end of that summer. I was heartbroken. I ended up losing my virginity on impulse at a sex party in a posh suburb of Paris, where women floated topless and hastily formed couples disappeared into the numerous bedrooms whose doors ran along the length of an interminable hallway. The guy was around forty, practiced in the art of picking up girls. I remembered nothing of him, neither face, body nor sex. Only that *it* was done painlessly, and perfunctorily. Just something to be done with, anonymously. He handed me a towel afterward, and I quickly got dressed and melted into the crowd, avoiding him for the rest of the night.

Years later I thought I had done it like that because it was a way of saying fuck you to men, not owing them anything, taking control of my sexuality.

41

ME: *WHAT ARE you doing this weekend?*

Him: *Going to the Hamptons.*

Me: *I thought you hated that crowd?*

Him: *I have a gig. A wedding.*

It was mid-June. An exceptionally hot and gorgeous June. I imagined him in his truck, windows open, stereo blasting. And I thought of Lena's empty cabin just above the beach, nestled in its lush setting of honeysuckle, the deck shadowed by the wisteria.

It was an impulse. I wasn't even sure Lena would be okay with it, although she had told me I was welcome to go whenever I wanted while she was in LA.

Him: *Really?*

I waited, heart beating. It was a gamble. Yes/No. Yes/No.

Him: *Cool. Maybe you can show me around.*

He picked me up late morning. His truck full to the gills—gear in the trunk and the backseat. He scooped up some random papers on the floor and tossed them to the back.

A/C? Windows open?

Windows.

I put my naked (freshly pedicured) feet up on the dashboard.

Cool toes.

I hoped it wouldn't suddenly dawn on him midway that I was sixty-two and what the hell was I doing in his car. But he shot a smile in my direction. I dropped my head down against the headrest and closed my eyes. I liked to be driven by him.

The cabin was sleepy. Shutters down. That musty smell of summer by the ocean before a house has been opened for the season. He picked up both our bags. Took the key from my hand as I was fumbling with it and figured out the lock. I quickly opened the shutters and the windows. The view was breathtaking—empty beach, gulls, and glittering ocean. Not a human in sight. He stepped out on the deck and stared off in the distance. He seemed more at ease here than he had been in my apartment, as if the presence of nature and the absence of neighbors liberated him. I put the groceries and the bottle of prosecco I had brought with me in the fridge. He went out to get his guitar and leant it against the wall.

He fell asleep after we had sex. Naked, his warm, damp skin fragrant with sweat and sperm. It was hot and humid, but we hadn't turned on the A/C, and a soft breeze blew in through the window screen. I gently ran my fingers over the hair curling on his chest. I thought of the American hippie boys I had slept with in the 70s when I had first come to New York. Was it all about trying to recapture that time? I remembered what it felt like to lie down with David in a hot New York summer, so close. Closer to anyone I had ever been with before and since.

We made sandwiches and went for a swim. The tide was up, licking the bottom of the dunes, the waves at an angle. The frigid water slapped us hard. When we got out, the ocean was starting to slip away. We found a dry spot on the dunes and lay down side-by-side on a towel I had found in the closet.

He scooped out some sand in his hand and spilled it over my naked navel, then blew it off gently. I had rolled the top of my bathing suit down to feel the sun on my chest and stomach. He leaned forward and licked each of my nipples.

I'm glad we came, he said.

What is the difference between lust and love? Can love lurk underneath the surface of desire? Can love be that feeling of pure presence in the world?

People started appearing on the beach, and we walked back up to the cabin.

We headed for the outdoor shower. He lathered me from head to toe. Even shampooed my hair. What was stopping us from being lovers for real?

You're adorable, he said.

Glass of chilled prosecco for the road?

Just a small one. The wedding is after sundown, but I've got to be there early to set up.

He got dressed. Tux, white shirt, black brogues.

No flip-flops? So, you keep a tux just for these events?

He did a full turn, arms akimbo.

How do I look?

You clean up good.

He picked up his guitar, still in its case.

What would it be like to be with him for real? I would write, live my life. Travel. Visit my granddaughter. Ha!

Are you going to wait for me?

Where would I go? I have a book to read. Mishima. Do you know who he is?

Japanese dude?

Yup. *The School of Flesh.* It's about a successful fashion designer who's having an affair with a much younger bartender—who happens to be a gay hustler as well.

He winced. Ouch! At least I am a cut above.

Don't flatter yourself.

Hey! Your age doesn't give you the right to be arrogant!

I was asleep when he came back, slipped into the bed. Whiskey and weed on his breath. His cock pushing against my butt.

In the morning we went for a swim, and he suggested brunch in a nearby ocean-side café. Maybe he was playing at being with me. I pushed the thought away. Why be cynical? It was a real date. He enquired about my preferences. Regular coffee or cappuccino, juice or no juice. Scrambled eggs or over easy. Smiled at me across the table. His card thrown into the tray. Suddenly he looked his age. 38. Silver in his hair. At that age, David and I had Juliet, owned an apartment. We made love in the afternoon. Ceiling fan full speed. Those New York summers I had fallen in love with, the first time I had landed at JFK at age twenty-two.

You know, when I told you about my ex-girlfriend, he said, pulling his arm from behind my shoulders. The German girl? Actually. She's my wife. Emma.

What!? You're married?

Yes. I mean, we are separated, but we are still officially married. Originally it was for the green card, but then it became more…

I was confused. Shocked, as though we had been carrying on a passionate love affair for months and were on the verge of moving in together, and he was revealing his dark secret. I had created a whole persona about him, a free spirit, never attached, hidden behind his iron clad irony. Perhaps even on the spectrum, and now this.

She was an artist, divorced from a wealthy businessman who still supported her and paid her rent. She had a big studio in Kreuzberg. Jonah'd lived there on and off for almost a year, but he hated being dependent on her. He had to come back to New York for his career. But even though she got her green card, her whole lifestyle was dependent on her ex-husband. She had to be in Berlin. They'd been together three years. Married for two.

She's older?

A little. Forty-five.

Are you still in touch?

We broke up a few months ago when I came back for good. But yeah. When I met you, in fact, she was in town. Are you upset?

No.

Why would I be upset? Because he was still married? Because she was older than him? Maybe that explained his attraction to me. I was grateful he had trusted me enough to open up. He had been hurt. He had taken chances in life. Had lived abroad. I had an urge to tell him about David, about Vadik. But it seemed futile. I had a sick feeling, as though the weekend had turned. And then I chased all these thoughts away. Who cared about memories? Anxiety about the future? Our bodies went for each other naturally, more freely than ever before, gripped in the urge to get close in spite of all that separated us.

We fell asleep in the sweltering afternoon, woke up to the chirp of a text on his cellphone. He sat up and cursed. He had forgotten he had a rehearsal. Nothing important, but still… I could see him hesitate. And type a quick response.

I said I was still in the Hamptons. Couldn't make it. They can rehearse without me.

I let myself relax. I was clinging to those last moments before heading back to the city. Let this weekend never end.

We sat on the deck. He picked up his guitar and played that sweet melody from his CD. "Ballad for Vida." Fireflies danced under the veranda. It was a fragile moment, blown glass that a gust of wind could break. He smiled at me, put the guitar down.

We went skinny dipping. Sunday night in June, the beach was deserted. We made love in the dunes and showered under the moonlight. It was full moon. A good omen. But of what. He entered me and carried me all the way to the bed, my thighs around his waist.

Your body fits perfectly with mine, he whispered. I could fall in love with you. Those were the last words I remembered of that night.

In the morning he was all business, perhaps embarrassed to have been weak the night before. He barely looked at me, and when he did it was from a far distance, almost surprised to find me here, this almost stranger in this strange place. How did that happen? He rushed for another shower, solo this time, packed his clothes, was the first to get to the car. But then I was surprised as well, as though the weekend had been a dream. We got coffee-to-go in town.

It was a muggy morning, the weather had turned on us, Highway 27 empty, straight between the potato fields. Sky hanging low. I clicked my window open and let the wind in with the smells of fresh-cut grass and brine.

He drove in silence. I was drowsy, still shot full of dopamine.

Eve.

To hear my name in his mouth, the V against his lip.

Don't take it the wrong way.

I sat up, pulled my feet down from the dash. Is there any way to take that line other than the wrong way? As anything but a flashing red light?

What?

It was an incredible weekend.

I knew what was coming. I couldn't stand another excuse, another lame justification. I had to protect myself, make the first move.

I felt a wave of adrenaline rise. The same wave that I had made me stand up to David and tell him to leave. It's over. Perhaps it was my ego, my armor. But I couldn't let Jonah crush me. Not now. I lied.

It was a great weekend. But I meant it when I said, "no strings attached." We don't owe anything to each other. Let's play it cool.

He shot me a sidelong glance. I could see the confusion mixed with relief on his face, or perhaps he was just surprised I was letting him off the hook so easily.

He took my hand and pressed it.

You're awesome.

42

LOUISE WANTED TO come over after work. She was reading for a new play, and she wanted to search through my closet, look for an outfit that would work for the part.

Sorry, I texted back. *I'm not alone tonight.*

And instantly felt a pinch of guilt. I was expecting him after six. Since our weekend in Montauk, he had spent the night at my place a few times. He'd pick up a beer in the fridge and sit at the kitchen table. I had wanted that intimacy between us, that everyday ease I had with Alan. That, for me, went deeper than candlelight and dates. At the same time, it unsettled me. Was I truly ready to open my home to Jonah? The simple idea of Louise meeting him made me nervous. But was it because I was afraid of her judgment, or because I wasn't sure of what I was doing?

I made an elaborate salad with quinoa and vegetables from the producers' market, whipped up a vinaigrette, placed two plates and glasses on the table, and cut slices of fresh bread. I didn't bother with a bottle of wine. We made do with beer. But even so it felt too formal, him sitting across the table from me. Too grown-up, as if we were kids playing house.

Have you ever been conned, or taken advantage of?

His question startles me.

We are lying side by side on my bed later that night. We have finally made it to the couch, then to the bedroom.

Why?

No reason.

Of course he must have a reason, but he won't say. Or perhaps the reason is semi-buried in his unconscious. I do that sometimes, blurt a question or a comment and then shut down. So I tell him about my trip to Algeria with David.

We had arrived by bus in an oasis village in the Sahara, and a young Berber merchant invited us to stay in his home in the middle of the medina, a small fortress of white-washed clay nestled in the center of town, beds and tables carved directly into the clay, and a flat roof on which a couple of goats lived and got milked in the morning for coffee. For fun one day, David showed Nasser how to make sand art in a couple of old Coca-Cola bottles. Impressed, Nasser brought the bottles and displayed them in the arcades of the hotel where all the tourists stayed, and they were a hit.

It's a long story, I warn Jonah, feeling again like Scheherazade, spinning tales to keep him in thrall. Go on, he says, his fingers in my hair.

Well, okay, it turned out that Nasser had a crush on the mayor's daughter, but being a lowly owner of a modest lingerie shop in the market, he had no hope of marrying her. But he had heard she admired the bottles and had asked her father to bring her one. Nasser asked David to make more bottles so that he could pretend that he had made them. As a would-be artist, he felt he had a better chance to earn the mayor's daughter's hand. But David had to swear he would not reveal the truth. In fact, he would have to promise to stay hidden in the house so no one would suspect foul play.

David agreed. It was a game. It was fun. David didn't take it seriously. Nasser would bring back sand from the desert and empty glass bottles of Coca-Cola at night, and in the morning, I would go to the market to buy natural dyes, and we would dye the sand on the rooftop next to the goats. David would make sand art in the bottles, and Nasser would bring them to the hotel to sell and pass them off as his. Every night Nasser pressured David to make more for the next day. And this went on for a few weeks until David couldn't stand it anymore, and he threatened to show up at the hotel and tell everyone he was the artist.

I pile up the details, how we had wanted to bring back Berber rugs to New York, and how David had negotiated a deal, Nasser arranging to have two Berber rugs given to us by his friend the carpet dealer, in exchange of our promise to keep complete silence. And how we had chosen the rugs and rolled them up and carried them attached to our backpacks all the way to Tunisia and back to New York via France, and how we had hung the rugs on the walls of our bedroom—which is the room where my office is now—but after a few months, moths started to fly over our heads when we were in bed, and we realized the rugs were full of moth larvae, and now they had hatched and the moths flew about and there were big holes in the rugs and we had to toss them out.

Ugh, gross, Jonah says. And what happened with Nasser and the mayor's daughter?

The girl was sitting at the terrace of the hotel with a mint tea and a pastry, Nasser fawning over her as we departed.

Ha-ha! Well done!

Huh. Kind of. Nasser got the girl of his dreams, and we were left with these shitty rugs!

Jonah laughs, and after a beat, he turns to me.

Eve. Emma's in town.

Emma? Your ex-wife?

Yes.

Is she staying with you?

She's staying with friends.

I remember that look he had had at the beginning of dinner, when I put down the salad on the table, how hesitant he had seemed as I invited him to sit down, and his sitting awkwardly, not pulling the chair all the way to the table, his body not settling down, like he had an urge to backtrack, but he was already way over his head, I thought we were past that already, on to the next phase, but now I can see his face shifting. And the silence that spreads between us is full of another life that I am not privy to.

43

I HAD GOTTEN the email from the French film producer after the weekend in Montauk. It was about a possible adaptation of my novel about David and I, *The way we lived.* After some back and forth, the producer had offered to pay for my plane ticket, and I jumped at the opportunity. That book had come out six years before, and I hadn't started a new project since I put aside the novella; the idea that my luck might be turning lifted my spirits. Plus it was Paris, and my first boyfriend, François, could put me up.

Jonah left for a cross-country tour, and I decided to start running to add cardio to my daily yoga. It was still that glorious time of the year in New York, cool in the early morning before the heat crushes the city. With age, I was convinced one has to up the ante, exercise-wise, in order to stay fit and healthy. I bought a pair of new running shoes to celebrate the good news. At seven a.m., I went running along the East River, joining the flow of young millennials working out before heading to their jobs downtown. And of course, because I believed in discipline—whether exercise or writing—I decided to go running every morning instead of easing into it.

Almost immediately, within a week or ten days, I started to feel tension in my left knee. If I alternated walking and running, it went away, so I kept walking on it. Maybe the knee would adjust. But after two weeks, I had to face the facts: my knee was hurt. My trusted osteopath, whom I went to consult all the way in Queens, diagnosed tendinitis and some stiffness in my left hip, and ordered me to wear an Ace bandage and to not walk more than ten minutes at a time.

How could I live if I couldn't walk? Ten minutes wouldn't even take me as far as the organic grocery store. He warned me to be patient. In a couple of weeks, I'd slowly start walking for longer periods and then I'd have to start working out with weights around my ankles to straighten my leg muscles while he worked on the tendon and the hip. I was going to France in a month, I protested. How long would it take until it's healed? I don't know, he said. Could be months. At your age, it takes longer to heal.

At my age.

I followed his orders religiously and bought adjustable cuff and ankle weights at Paragon. By the time I was ready to go to France, I could walk thirty minutes. Not nearly enough, but it would have to do.

Louise assessed me sternly.

You're limping, Mom. Is it wise of you to go to Paris like that? Maybe you need a cane? Don't hesitate to ask for a wheelchair at the airport.

I caught the sly smile hovering about her lips and we both burst out in laughter,

What about the weights? I asked the osteopath. I can't bring them to Paris with me!

Just strap plastic bottles of water around your ankles. It'll work just as well.

I forgot to say he was from Romania. They learnt how to be very can-do over there, when they lived on the other side of the Iron Curtain.

44

THERE WAS A heat wave in Paris. It was the new normal in France, days of brutally high temperature rendered even more suffocating by the lack of air conditioning in most buildings or even in most subway stations and buses, in a city coiled around itself in a labyrinth of narrow streets, historically accustomed to a more moderate climate. It didn't feel like the heat in New York, always humid and tropical, from which you could find shelter in refrigerated stores and cars, or in the ocean breeze rushing down the canyons of the avenues, but like a malevolent sauna—Rome without the lush vegetation and the whiff of jasmine and honeysuckle in the air.

In the windows, lit up by the bright sun, my hair took on strange orangey tones. The mirrors at Monoprix, where I took refuge to try on some lingerie in a relatively cool air, reflected the softening of my jaw with an evil intent, while the overhead light revealed paler roots in my hair, as if the dressing room had been designed for maximum humiliation. Even my abs took on unflattering shadows and my breasts—I would swear—hung lower than they had in New York. Not to mention my knee was still tender!

Each time I went to Paris, a town that I professed to love with an eternal love, all my childhood and teenage years rushed back into the glare of my present: the socially awkward, gangly, unhip, shy, geeky girl I had been, ashamed of my rebellious, wild mother, of my absent father. As I walked out of the dressing room, struggling with the bra hangers, a man glanced at me, and I fled.

I walked a few blocks to the elegant Le Bon Marché, where I asked to be perfumed with a spray of my new favorite scent, Sables by Annick Goutal. The mist of bergamot and vanilla enveloped me and marginally put me back together. When I looked at myself in the mirrors of the store, more softly lit, I was walking a little straighter, a little more self-assured, like Alice after eating from the other side of the mushroom.

I was staying at François's barely fixed up loft, under the rafters, near République. I would take care of his cat while he was traveling.

The night before he left, he invited me to a restaurant tucked away behind Église Saint-Vincent de Paul in the 10th arrondissement. On the way, boulevard Magenta, we walked past a homeless couple having sex in the middle of the sidewalk, barely covered by a blanket that was suggestively writhing and twisting in the sweltering evening.

Paris is turning into New York, I said. In fact, I had never seen anyone fucking in the streets of New York, only urinating or defecating. I took a step aside, disturbed by the spectacle of the couple wiggling under the blanket.

I was supposed to meet the film producer the next day to discuss the adaptation of my novel. It was the story of a woman, a performance artist, whose husband fell in love with another woman. The man is a struggling painter, the lover a famous gallerist. He goes back and forth between the two women until the wife, unable to take it any longer, shoots him in the heart at a gallery opening, and then tries to pass off the murder as a performance piece. I met the producer at the Deux Magots café, on boulevard Saint-Germain. The heat wave had broken, and it was raining. The rain or the prospect of talking about my work had washed out my insecurity of the morning at Monoprix, and I had regained some self-confidence.

We sat outside, under the awning dripping with rain, surrounded by Parisians who'd rather be wet and smoking than dry and tobacco-less. The American tourists were all huddled inside. The producer saw the potential screenplay as a neo-nouvelle-vague flick, black and white with an experimental jazz score. When I read his notes later, I found out he had issues with almost every scene, and with the three main characters.

But right now, I was floating on a sea of contentment, and entertained the idea of asking Jonah if he might be interested in writing the music. I even accepted a cigarette from the producer, although I hadn't smoked in decades. I was at ease, here, speaking my native language, in the neighborhood where I had gone to college, far from the suburbs where I had grown up. The streets shiny with rain. The small French cars driving by in the shwoosh of wet tires. The rattan chairs, the waiters with their long aprons, the angular water carafes with SUZE written in art deco lettering on yellow background. Paris frozen in time—not the time of my childhood, but the eternal time of film.

After dinner, when the rain tapered off, I walked all the way back to République without hurting my knee, but I had to hold on to the banister to climb the steep staircase of François's building up to the sixth floor. I stood at the open window overlooking the gray zinc roofs glassy with rain in the long Paris early summer twilight, restless, frustrated.

I went to bed late, unable to sleep with the jet lag. Idly thumbing my cellphone, I clicked on the dating site icon, and, on a lark, changed my location to Paris. No strings attached, I had firmly repeated to Jonah when he left for his tour. It was no time to chicken out and romanticize our affair. A few minutes later, *iParis,* 40, software engineer, sent me a message. He liked high heels, stockings, and garters. He was cute and it was fun to flirt in French—and do a comparison study of American vs. French men. He wanted to meet me in a café that very night, although he didn't offer to pick me up on his *moto* because the rain had picked up again. It was already one in the morning and pouring. I turned him down.

The next morning, *Archi18*, 29, architect, contacted me. The sun was shining again, and he suggested afternoon café near the Abbesses subway station, which was much more appealing than a seedy date in the middle of the night under the rain. I promptly forgot *iParis* and got ready to meet *Archi18*, wearing a short, flowered dress and sandals. I took the subway in order not to have to walk too much. My knee was a bit weak but holding up.

He was waiting for me, tall, with dark hair and deep blue eyes. It was delicious to have a date with a cute French architect in a Montmartre café, like a tourist in my hometown. He was from Dijon. His name was Xavier. It was a beautiful Sunday afternoon, and we were surrounded by young Parisians settling down to an afternoon of espresso or Perrier, chatting, flirting, and people watching. I felt like a character in a film, considering a slightly risky affair. The age difference was even more staggering than with Jonah, but I liked the edge it gave me. An hour later, after we said goodbye, he texted me *Vous êtes charmante*, which was more seductive than the abrupt and direct American *Hey! Shall we get together?* Of course the use of the formal *"vous"* added to the appeal. It had an old-fashioned ring to it, especially charming coming from a twenty-nine-year-old.

Xavier texted me on and off the next couple of days, trying to arrange a proper date in his apartment up on the Montmartre Hill. His texts were sweet and often ending with *Je t'embrasse,* and other adorable flirty niceties. I was stoked for the date, which we agreed on for the next evening at eight p.m. But when the time came to get ready and head to his place, I realized that, although I had his address and floor number, I didn't know his *digicode*, the code that you must type in to enter any apartment building in Paris.

He apologized. His parents had unexpectedly shown up from Dijon and would stay at his place the whole weekend. He was so, so sorry. Could we reschedule later in the week?

I burst into laughter. Maybe twenty-nine *was* too young, if he still had to deal with his parents, who probably had bought him his apartment in Montmartre, one of the hottest old neighborhoods of Paris. Or maybe he had gotten cold feet. That older woman/younger man trend was a seductive one, especially in France, but he may have thought better to keep it as fantasy.

At midnight, French time, as I was about to fall asleep, my phone pinged. Jonah. In the dark, his message popped neon bright.

Are you back?

A burning ember caught fire in my stomach. It was six p.m. in New York, the time he usually left the studio. That meant he was back in town. His name was a promise of bliss, barely held together by these three little words *Are you back,* that might vanish as soon as his attention would go back to his music or alight on another object of desire. I didn't answer, but kept the message on my screen without opening the phone, like a talisman carved into an ancient stone. The message was still there when I woke up, the late morning sun pushing its way around the curtains.

The next day I was headed to Switzerland to visit my godfather, who was recovering from a heart attack. In the high-speed train cutting southeast through green pastures and clusters of farms flipping by in fast-forward, I kept the three little words *Are you back* on my screen. It's only when I got back to Paris, two days later, that I answered.

Still in Paris, I wrote. And I hit send.

45

IT WAS AN in-between time, this back to New York at the end of August. Fall was already falling over Paris, cool evenings, jackets, and scarfs, while landing at JFK in the middle of the night waiting for a taxi in the suffocating heat was a rewind to the heart of the summer. I loved that sultry heat, its sensuality, the way your body lets go and its contours soften and melt into the humid air, and the brain loses its deadly grip on your emotions. And in that in-between time, too, before Labor Day and even way after, the heat went on pummeling, the A/C on at night, the ceiling fans whirring, and the desire for Jonah swelled in me with the heat, Jonah so close to me and yet invisible, beyond reach. I hadn't heard from him since I got back.

46

I WAS HAVING dinner with Lena at a sidewalk café in the Lower East Side. As we sipped our sauvignon blanc, waiting for the salads we had ordered, it occurred to me that I had met Jonah almost a year ago, just after my birthday. If this had been a romance, one year would have been a milestone, when it starts to take on the firmer contour and the rituals of a relationship. Of course, our affair was just as nebulous as ever, our encounters, scattered small islands that only appeared at low tide, always threatening to be engulfed.

If you still see him after a year, he'll stick around, Lena said. Otherwise, he would have been long gone. Lena was the eternal optimist, in spite of, or maybe because of being a veteran of complicated affairs.

I shook my head. Maybe. But he's a distraction from my writing. Going down the rabbit hole of nostalgia. Trying to relive the first years with David or something… The archetype of the American artist that I fell for back then. Whatever.

Lena was the one who had first signed up on the dating site to get over a failed romance, and I had followed out of curiosity. Besides, nobody our age ever met anybody in real life anymore. Millennials and Gen. Z were all over Tinder, Bumble, Hinge. Hardly anyone spoke or approached each other in real life for fear of being perceived as creepy. The same guy you met at a cocktail party and who barely talked to you might contact you online and—within these newly defined boundaries—be all over you and madly making out with you at the back of a dark bar. Lena had not found anyone interesting, and I was the one who had lucked out, if one could say "lucking out" about Jonah. But in a way, I had. As Alan had said, looking at Jonah's picture, whistling between his teeth, he was *choice.*

Just then Lena's phone pinged.

Speaking of the devil, she said. New message.

She clicked on the icon and waited for the profile to download.

A young one. Thirty-eight. Really cute. Look.

She handed me her phone. The cellphone, harbinger of bliss or heartbreak. The picture was a different one. Not the one where he was wearing a sports coat over a graphic T-shirt, a bushy beard, a guitar on his knees, which had won me over. On this one he looked younger, in a bright red T-shirt, just a stubble of a beard, and his guitar against his chest. Maybe it was a promotional band photo.

We read his message together. It was, word for word, the same message he had sent me the first time: "*Hi, I'm Jonah, you seem quite lovely.*"

The next day, when I logged on the site, he had deactivated his profile again.

47

HELLO, I'M GENERAL Ralph Omero. You seem to be the perfect woman for me. Thanks.

EasyRider, 34 – You are just stunningly sexy.

Coolboy, 58 – Such a beautiful sexy woman hope you like my profile

SmilefromRome, 45 – Hi nice woman, a kiss from Rome

BooNJ, 25 – Hey, any fun plans this weekend, you're gorgeous.

Ilovemature – I can bang you good

Toyboy69 – Hi my mistress. I'll do anything you want, be your servitor. I am sub slave and my name is Adam but you may call me bicht, asslicker or anything else. … I live in brooklyn near prospect park. Dont have any limits of controlling me. Before i had mistress in russia and i served to her for long time. I like to do massage, wash panties, cook, shave legs, pussy, ass. My fantasy is To be humiliation by mistress. I like to wash my mistress in bath. First tribute is to serve to my mistress and do everything she says. I wish to serve you very well also i wish to serve you friends when they come to your home. Also you can give me for rent for your friends. I am also interested in cuckold hubby relationship and ready for it. We can go to bar and have a drink and see what happens, maybe i will lick your ass and pussy in the restroom of the bar. Thanks for reading my mistress.

Toyboy69's thumbnail showed a silhouette dressed in a shapeless white robe, kneeling on a bare floor, face obscured by a white oval, a washcloth in his hand, scrubbing away. Another picture showed his hand holding a delicate, well-groomed foot, about to dip it into a basin of foamy water.

48

YOU KNOW SEBALD? What a surprise!

MackTheKnife, 42, Edinburg is a Sebald scholar from Berlin. Lost in the Scottish highlands. Not too many pretty girls in the University of Edinburg, I figure. Good pic. Early forties. Strong, sensual, Germanic face. Brutal? Just a hint. Oh, those Germans. Just a step away from going overboard. *Do you like anal sex?* It's an epidemic. All thanks to porn. Before online dating, they'd keep it under wraps until they felt they could spring it on you. Anal used to be an exotic transgression. Now it's an opening line. Online, all the fetishes are out on the open. *It depends. With the right person at the right time in the right mood,* I answer. *But you would?* He insists. *Maybe.* I text back.

He's thousands of miles away. It's just virtual sexy talk with strangers. I would, with him, right now, if he turned me on to it. *Ever use a plug?* He asks. *Huh, no. Bit too technical for me. Don't like toys and tools*, I text back. I think German = BDSM. Is that being stereotypical? But I like sex talk. It's a cheap turn-on. *There are these girls I do it with*, he continues, *they are as open at the back as in front. Then I have them suck my dick afterwards.*

I know. I know. But it doesn't sound as crude as it seems. He's a Sebald scholar, for God's sake. It gives the whole convo an air of intellectualism and refinement. Plus he writes well. His English is colloquial. Just the right slang. I settle down on my bed, my laptop next to me. He tells me all in great detail what he would do to me, me to him, the little chat window popping open at the speed of light, while I contribute just enough hmmm and yea... to keep him going, which doesn't take much. He's lost in his dream. *Are you excited?* He asks. It's the new version of phone sex. Because the written words address the imagination without the heavy and cumbersome presence of a human voice. Online sex goes straight to the essential. We finish almost at the same time. Me, right after him, my fingers deep into my wet crotch. *Did you like? Want to do it again?* I let his question hang without answering. I'm done with him. I shut down my computer, turn off the light and go to sleep.

49

I HAD BEEN working on my screenplay all day when his text popped up. My plan was to send the French producer a new draft by the end of October. Adapting your own novel for the screen is a challenge, but it's engrossing to pull apart the structure and test if it's solid enough to turn into a film. Play with the dialogue. Pare it down.

He was still on. That's the first thought I had. If I answered, I could have him, right now. I was alone in the apartment. In a few minutes, he would be running up the stairs as he had done so many times... the desire was suffocating. But I remembered his picture on Lena's phone and his message. *Hi, you seem quite lovely...* Those charming words I naively thought had been written just for me. Louise wouldn't have fallen for that. Not only was I way older than Jonah, but I was also a novice at online dating, novice in the ways of hook-up culture. Then I remembered him naked on my bed the first time, his smile almost shy. Apologizing for not being a "good rebound guy." Him on the bed of the Montauk cabin saying, "I could fall in love with you." For all his cheeky comebacks, his cool façade, he wasn't sure how to handle me, an older woman, more sophisticated, more worldly... And I didn't know how to read him. We didn't speak the same language. I fantasized being Colette, the older, established writer keeping a young lover in thrall. What was *his* fantasy?

I stood at the window. Under the rays of the setting sun, the new plants I had acquired since I had met him—in a movement of optimism, of life renewal—were thriving, lush and green. They were turning into a little jungle. I waited until the impulse to text him back passed and went back to my screenplay.

50

DO YOU STILL like that book now?

Louise is checking the books piled on my desk and spots a novel written by a writer who has just been accused of sexual harassment by a former student.

I still like it, I say, and remember, you liked it more than I did. You said it was a *very good* book. I thought it was too long at times. But an important voice.

Are you still going to assign it to your students?

Probably. I don't believe in banning the work because the author has made mistakes. Some of my favorite writers had questionable opinions and actions. The great French writer, Céline, was an avowed anti-Semite, for instance. In fact, it would be a good opportunity to discuss the issue with the students. Don't you agree?

She thinks for a moment then shakes her head.

No, I don't. He shouldn't be rewarded.

Louise is always ready to rush the barricades to fight for women's rights.

She also closely monitors my dating life.

I don't think this guy is treating you well.

Who are you talking about?

You know.

Oh. Him. It's over anyway.

You always say that. And then you keep seeing him. Are you putting yourself out there?

Since when are daughters talking as if they are the mothers?

Didn't you meet anybody you liked on that dating site? Someone you could seriously get involved with? How many people have you met?

Dozens… okay, no. At least twenty, more likely.

Incredulous, Louise opens her eyes wide. And you didn't like any of them? How could you not have liked any of those guys? You need to lower your standards.

That makes me laugh.

Actually, it's not true. I did like one. Sorry, two.

Two! Gee, mom!

Stop it! An orchestra conductor. And a film director. I really liked the orchestra conductor. About my age, maybe a little younger. A grown daughter. Really interesting guy. Cool. My type of guy.

What happened?

He wasn't into me. I guess. We emailed back and forth and then… nothing.

Why?

I shrug. I don't know. It's okay. Things don't always work out. Men my age often look for younger women.

Louise makes a sad face. Are you happy?

I know the questioning comes from love. Louise as a concerned Jewish mother fretting over her offspring. But to me, it feels like running the gauntlet.

I think happiness is overrated, I say, making a poor stab at humor.

Louise's face tenses up. Suddenly she looks like my mother.

I hate it when you're fake.

There was a passage I had underlined in my battered copy of Joan Didion's *Play it as it Lays* after David had left. I don't remember the exact words, but it was about women standing in the checkout line at the supermarket, buying just a lamp chop for themselves and some cat food on Saturday evenings. The ignominy of the single, divorced woman.

For years, I avoided the Saturday morning Union Square greenmarket where we used to shop every week together, because it was wall-to-wall families or couples and it was too unbearably painful. It took a while, but eventually I joined the ranks of countless divorcees who—consciously or not—had sworn off relationships. And I had perfected the art of shopping for one to the point that when Louise came over, she banged fridge and cupboards doors open and shut, complaining that there was never anything to eat in the house.

One night after he moved out, David had offered to babysit Louise when I went out, but when I came back much later than planned, he was furious. We had a fight.

It's for the best that we broke up, I told him. Our life was stifling me.

Livid, he threw me on the couch and unbuckled his belt, pulled down his jeans to enter me.

No, I said. No! What the fuck are you doing!

I pushed him away, and he stumbled back into his pants.

You're all bravado, he said. You don't mean any of this.

He was so angry, he tore the laundry room closet door off its hinges on his way out and grabbed me by the arm so hard I had a red mark for days after that. He had to come back a few days later to fix the door.

51

CHRISTMAS AGAIN.

Jonah had tried me once more, sometime after Thanksgiving, and I had heroically refrained from answering. It would have been our second Christmas, I thought secretly, even though I knew I was the only one counting. Jonah had awakened a throbbing phantom limb. I toiled away at the dinner, the tree majestic, wrapped in garlands of white lights and blown glass ornaments, Louise piling the presents on the red velvet piece of cloth draped at the base of the tree. Everyone sitting around the table, Vivian already in bed. The glazed Virginia ham passed around, and later the Yule log stabbed with tiny marzipan mushrooms and colorful dwarves.

There was no text from him this time. No playful request for a photo.

The day before I had gone to get the bagels at the new place he had once recommended, and we had them for breakfast along with croissants from a French bakery. Covering all cultural bases.

The bagels were small and crisp, hand-made, without too much dough. The way they must have been made when the Jews first arrived to America fleeing the Russian and East European pogroms at the turn of the previous century. They tasted like those David and I bought at Schwartz's on boulevard Saint-Laurent in Montreal when we lived there.

My ex-mother-in-law taught me to cut the fresh bagels in halves and freeze them, so that if you pull them out of the freezer and pop them in the toaster, they come out tasting as fresh as the day they were baked. She also taught me how to make chicken soup, with the onion pierced with four cloves at exactly right angles—north, south, east, and west.

But everything else had fallen by the wayside, Hanukkah, and the menorah with the candles, lit up one day at a time, seders and the bitter herbs, the gold coin hidden for the kids to go look for it. The yarmulkes on the men's heads—miraculously perched, whether on a full head of hair or on a bald skull—at bar-and bat-mitzvahs, weddings, and funerals. The gefilte fish and the potato latkes. The chopped liver. *What am I? Chopped liver?* These expressions I learnt from David, and I was surprised to discover that not every American was familiar with, or used those turns of phrase, or even got their humor. What I had thought was American culture was New York Jewish-American culture.

The day after Christmas, Juliet came out of her bedroom scratching her upper arms. Three little dots, bite-like, dotted her right bicep, although not in a row.

Do these look like bedbugs bites to you?

We all convened into the living room for a war meeting and inspection of the bites. Vivian jumped up and down. Wanna see. Wanna see. Scott picked her up so that she could have a good look at the bites.

Don't! Don't sit on the couch!

Louise's boyfriend broke down. There was a bedbug scare a few days ago in his apartment, he confessed. He got bitten. His landlord called an exterminator. They didn't find anything but….

Louise turned against him in a rage. And you didn't tell me? You came here and slept in the bed with me? And you sat on the couch last night?

We all inspected our arms, our necks. Conflicting information flew off. The bites have to be in a row. They are never on the legs, or always on the arms and torso. Close-ups of bites stared at us from our phones. We compared the pictures against Juliet's arms.

They could be spiders. Remember when we had a spider infestation in that bedroom? And all these tiny bites you had?

The man came the next morning. Without a dog. The more reliable option was a man with a dog, but it was pricey. I cut corners and hired a man by himself, minus the dog, from another company. He was an elderly gentleman from Turkey. He upended the mattresses in each bedroom, pulled the couch from the wall.

We waited, huddled in the middle of the room, not daring to sit anywhere, for our fate to be decided.

The man shook his head. Then he looked at the bites on Juliet's arm.

Nope, he said.

Are you sure?

He lifted his baseball hat, which bore the name of his extermination company and made him look incongruously American in contrast to his old-world demeanor, thought for a moment, placed it back atop his thick gray hair, and looked me straight in the eyes.

Been in this business for fifty years. Never made a mistake. I know these little buggers. Can't miss'm. You don't have'm.

We all laughed. We wanted to hug the man who brought us a few days of bliss. We couldn't believe we had dodged that bullet.

52

THE FENG SHUI lady came the day after I found out the small townhouse adjacent to my building was set to be demolished. The townhouse had belonged to an elderly lady who lived on the ground floor and rented the upper ones. When she passed away, her heirs sold the property for top dollar to a developer. Intent on maxing out his investment, the developer wanted to replace the house with a condo built, as New York City laws allowed, right next to the property line of my building.

My stomach clenched in a knot at the idea of losing my spring and summer views of the ivy creeping on the building wall across the garden and of two ailanthus trees growing in two adjacent lots which would be occulted. By an ironic circling back of fate, gentrification was bringing the neighborhood back to its dense urban fabric.

Small and slight with long, dark hair cut across her forehead in severe bangs, Wang Jing assured me the loss of the view wouldn't affect the feng shui and handed me a colorful sheet of paper. The *bagwa.* It was an octagonal grid superimposed on the layout of my apartment. It turned out that only my study was well balanced, with its old farm table that served as a desk standing in the relationship corner, while another table on which I did my paperwork was properly located in the wealth corner. The living room didn't fare as well. Couch in the wrong corner, facing the wrong way. We were about to walk in my bedroom when Wang Jing looked up.

Oh my God! She jumped aside as if she had glimpsed a spider hanging from the ceiling. She pointed to a huge film poster of

Martin Scorcese's *Goodfellas* thumbtacked to the wall of the hallway. The poster was in French, retitled *Les Affranchis.*

Do you see what I'm seeing, she asked. Look at these three guys. They're like sentinels guarding your bedroom and stopping any man from getting involved with you.

The poster was my ex-husband's, I said sheepishly.

Why had I kept everything just as David had left it? Everything was frozen in time. The only room I had completely made mine was the study.

Walking into my bedroom, Wang Jing pointed to a charcoal drawing of a naked woman taking her bath, and a black and white photo of a girl standing alone in the rain holding an umbrella.

These have to go. Pictures of single women no good in a bedroom. Only pictures of you. And these are your daughters?

I laughed. I got where Wang Jing was going with that.

A woman's bedroom wasn't for the mother but for the lover, she said. Which might explain my love life, cobbled together as an afterthought. She suggested a different kind of artwork instead: a man and a woman embracing, two birds, or other animals as a pair. Pairs sent the right messages to the universe. I cringed. A pair of cooing birds? So cheesy! Oh, and don't pack up your drawers and closets too much; you need to make room for a potential mate in your life.

After Wang Jing left, I removed the offending artwork and replaced it with a postcard of the famous *Kiss* by Doisneau. What better image to conjure love than a pair of lovers kissing in Paris? Finally, I placed two red hearts made of glass on a windowsill in the relationship corner, flanked by two candlesticks, for good measure.

I was barely done when there was a text from Jonah.

Hi Eve, are you around after work? I miss you.

53

HOW ABOUT A drink? Time for a quick one? Scotch on the rocks?

I was nervous, fussing at the kitchen counter, the tension between us thick. I poured some scotch in a glass and handed it to him neat.

What about the rocks? He flashed his sexy smile, his eyebrows going up a little.

I smiled back and took the ice tray out of the freezer.

It's been a long time, he said.

Yes.

You kept ignoring my texts. You meet somebody?

If I did, do you think I would tell you?

Touché.

He walked over to the piano and sat on the bench, lifted the lid.

Beautiful sound. Even out of tune, I can tell how warm the tone it is. I never played on an antique piano before. And the ivory keys!

He played a few more notes, but they were too discordant. Then he sat down next to me on the couch. I could tell he hesitated whether to make a move or not.

I've been thinking a lot about you since the summer.

He put his hand on my knee, searched my eyes.

Before he came, I had sworn to myself that I would play it cool—cold even. But a ball of anger exploded in my chest, spread around my neck, up to my cheeks.

Eve?

Oh yeah? If I was so special to you, why did you go straight to the site when I came back from France, and contacted Lena? My friend Lena. We stayed in her cabin in Montauk.

What? What are you talking about?

Yes, you sent her a message when I was with her, sitting across from her. She showed me your picture. We were having dinner in a little outdoor restaurant.

He looked stunned. I have no idea what you're talking about.

Of course, you have no idea. You don't know her. You just clicked on her picture. It was one summer night after you came back from your tour. Remember? Or do you click on so many women's pictures they're all a blur to you?

I hated myself for revealing my jealousy, for berating him like a possessive wife. But it was too late now. I peeled his hand off my knee and pulled away from him on the couch.

He was looking at me, unsure how to react. Dumbfounded to have walked into a scene. Not what he expected from me, the cool older woman I had played so far.

You're right, I don't remember. I'm sorry. What a crazy coincidence. But…

Now I felt embarrassed. I thought of Genwittstein, the German guitar player I had been thrilled to sleep with because Jonah probably knew him. Online dating, the meat market, where you're bound to run into everybody you knew or used to know. You log on mindlessly at night and cruise the photos, leave messages that you immediately forget. Hadn't I myself stumbled upon the picture of an architect I had dated a few years earlier, and of a married musician I had flirted with while spending a summer at a writer's residency? Everybody was there, risking getting caught red-handed, trying out fresh meat. I felt a wave of nausea. Jonah wasn't the problem. It was that game we were engaged in. That I had no control over.

I can leave if you want.

No. Stay. It's all right.

He took my hand and pressed it hard.

I'm sorry. I've no idea what I am doing. You may have noticed.

He leaned over and kissed me. We made love on the couch and in my room, and he spent the night. In the morning, I made coffee and took out the French country bread I always kept in the bread box and we sat down at my kitchen table like a newly in love couple, and I forgot about the past pressing so hard around me in the apartment. I realized how much I craved this intimacy, this sweet domesticity when you've made love with a man and you get ready for your day, when you're simply present to your life.

54

THE SONG POPPED up on my phone the next day. No text. Just the little triangle to click on.

I was having lunch at the Cornelia Street café with François who was visiting New York for a few days, and another old friend from Paris.

Is that a new beau? they asked, seeing me fuss with my phone.

Sort of.

Show us.

I scrolled around to show them the picture that was on the cover of one of his CDs, in which he looked like a movie star.

They whistled.

Sexy, said one. Pretty boy, said the other.

I rushed back home to listen to the song.

It was a guitar solo, more melodic than what I had heard on his clips.

Slow and languorous, tender, even. My heart melted a little. It was sweet, like the *hi, sweetie* he had greeted me with one time. Completely unexpected.

Sweet, I texted him back.

55

LOUISE ASKS TO meet me in a small English tearoom where we used to go every Wednesday afternoon after school after David left. We order what we used to order: a tea and scones for me, and a high tea for Louise, which we will share.

We eat the little watercress and tuna sandwiches and the scones, coated with clotted cream. On the tiny table, a teapot in the shape of a gingerbread house is surrounded with pots of milk, sugar, and floral china. My mother used to take me to a tearoom in Paris, near where she worked as a fashion designer's assistant. It was on the second floor of the English bookstore WHS Smith, at the corner of rue Cambon and rue de Rivoli, with a view on the Tuileries.

Since home was a war zone, each camp armed to the teeth on either side of the trenches, the only good times between me and my mother took place in tea rooms, department stores, concerts, ballet shows, plays, and the occasional vacation. The tea room ritual was the best. Starched, straw-yellow tablecloth and napkins, silver teapots, and milk. Clicking of delicate silverware against china. Hushed voices. Scents of bergamot, lemon. Swirls of spicy English cigarettes smoke. My mother elegant, pencil skirt, silk blouse, clip-on earrings, short platinum wavy hair with two kiss curls, a beauty spot at the corner of her lips, Madame Rochas perfume.

Here the ambiance is more English country inn. Crowded elbow to elbow on minuscule tables and flowery tablecloths. We keep refilling our cups of tea and nibbling on tea sandwiches until Louise takes me by surprise.

She felt abandoned after the divorce, she says, always alone in her room after school while I was locked into my study, writing.

My office has no door, I say, lamely. It's open to the rest of the apartment.

Louise shrugs. Don't be so literal. You know what I mean.

Sharp arrows aimed straight at my heart. The hour of reckoning when your daughter presents you with her list of grievances. I did the same with my mother.

I helped you with your homework. I was with you. I was there.

When? You were always working. Spending your time with imaginary characters instead of in real life.

I had to write to support us.

I always have the same answer: I'm working. But I'm lying. The whole living room was teeming with ghosts. The family theater was still being played in reruns. The air still thick with the sounds of old sitcoms, fights, and heavy silences. My study was my refuge from the crushing emptiness left by David's exit, as if he alone had filled the apartment with his male presence, his body moving molecules around with a different kind of energy. Afterward, the three of us, Juliet, Louise, and I, were alone clutching the rafter at sea. And then Juliet started college. And it was just Louise and me. But if I am honest, I was afraid I wouldn't know how to reassure Louise, I felt too shaky to be the strong mother she needed. It was easier to take cover in my study. At least there, surrounded by my notebooks, my writing, I held on to myself. The guilt is so strong I can barely breathe.

My therapist says you should have sent me to therapy right after the divorce, Louise continues. She says divorced moms often refuse to see the psychological problems of their children because they are so intent on showing that they can raise them on their own.

It's a punch through my stomach. All the mistakes I've made, all my shortcomings rise like a huge mountain.

I thought you'd be okay. You were not even six.

But I know the therapist is right. I was determined to show David I could keep it together, contrary to what he might have thought. His words, still living in my head: emotionally unbalanced, weak, afraid of my own shadow, dysfunctional. Neurotic. Because the alternative. They take children away from crazy mothers. My mother's words: your grandparents wanted to denounce me as an unfit mother, adopt you legally, my mother screams, tears of rage brimming in her eyes. Can you imagine? The bastards!

Once, decades after the facts, I confronted her in her bedroom overlooking the Estérel hills in Provence. You weren't there when I was growing up. Mamie and Papy were the ones who took care of me. She protested. I was working during the day. I wanted to leave, but I always came back. I didn't want to abandon you. They made life hell for me. But they loved you. My mother's voice was shaky, pleading, her eyes wild with guilt. Out of rage, my hands flew around her neck. I pressed hard with my thumbs. With relish, I noted the terror in her eyes. Now, the memory of her green, devastated eyes is unbearable.

Are you upset that I said that? Louise asks.

Yes. I look down. My eyes are filling with tears.

Louise crumbles her scone with her fork.

What? You aren't going to cry now, are you? Stop it. Don't play the victim. See, you're still self-centered. It's not about you.

56

WANG JING CAME back with a report of what needed to be done to bring my apartment up to feng shui speed. As she had been with my bedroom, she was radical with the rest of the apartment. The living room was all wrong. The couch was cramped in the money corner, while the piano clung to the relationship side of the room with all the stubbornness of its big-pawed, elephantine legs. A 1930 baby grand, with a pattern of inlaid mother-of-pearl running around the bent side squatted in the living room like a dinosaur from my past, shipped at great cost from France, evidently stopping new relationships from blossoming.

I bought silicone sliders to put under the feet of the piano so it could be pushed across the room without damaging the floor. With Louise and Alan, who had just come back with his visa, we huffed and puffed, pushed, and pulled and cleared the space for the couch, while the piano sailed to the other end of the living room.

Well… the piano is in the wealth corner now, I said, consulting the bagwa. I doubt it'll bring an improvement to my finances.

You'll either have to sell it for a lot of money or start playing again, Alan said.

And become a successful jazz pianist?

You could ask *Jazzman* to come and play. Or he could come and noodle his guitar and bring a pianist friend.

Louise made a face at the mention of *Jazzman*.

I went to the piano and sat at the old bench, whose velvet upholstery was ripped and ragged. I opened the lid. The keys felt warm. They were real ivory, not those plastic-covered ones they make nowadays since ivory has been banned to protect the elephants. I caressed the veins with my fingers.

I tried the right hand. The scales, the simplest. Perhaps, like riding a bicycle, you don't forget.

Okay. Can you play something else now?

I closed the lid. My music sheets were piled on a shelf, so old the paper was crumbling at the edges. Perhaps, in another life. if I had taken a different path…

I'll have someone come and tune it.

That evening, I played again but with Louise. Play it again, Sam. Play it again, Eve. My fingers started to pick up a rhythm. I could hear the languor of a Chopin waltz. But forget about Chopin. It's Bill Evans I wanted to hear. I see Jonah standing by the piano with his guitar strapped to his chest like a rocker. There would be the drums at the back, and he would slay, he would shred and slide and groove and slink around the beat.

It was a family room when David lived here, the TV on all day Sunday, college basketball, baseball, NFL, World Series, Superbowl, world championship boxing, family videos, *The Cosby Show*, and *60 Minutes*, all on the small, antiquated Sony, and then the play dates, the kids' parties, the strawberry shortcakes thick with fresh whipped cream, and Happy Birthday drawn in glossy red with a special pastry bag fitted with a small tip.

You can still play, mom!

I closed the lid.

Not for real. Not without hours and hours of practice. I think that ship has sailed.

57

A BLISTERING MONDAY. We stood in front of each other in my bedroom, dressed almost the same. In jeans and T-shirt. On his way, he had texted me: *Can I dress you?* I was excited by the idea. Now I was waiting for his instructions.

Button-down?

I opened my closet and showed him my shirts. A chocolate silk one, a navy blue cotton one, a pale blue chambray one, a black one, and a crisp, white one.

I placed each in front of me, modeling them. He studied each one at length.

This one, he said, pointing to the white one.

I slowly removed my tee and buttoned the shirt all the way to my neck.

Now off with the jeans. He was having trouble keeping a straight face.

I stood before him with my naked legs.

So?

Tights?

I took a pair of sheer tights from my lingerie drawer and slipped them on. It was sexy under the white shirt buttoned up to my neck. And the glasses. He hesitated.

How about this? He pulled out a miniskirt from its hanger.

I could see his erection.

Pumps? Boots?

He slowly shook his head.

No. Like this.

I cupped him into my palm, through the fabric of the pants.

He sucked in his breath and leaned into me, pressed his mouth against mine.

We dragged the comforter in front of the big mirror.

Look, he said. Look at us in the mirror.

But I wasn't watching. I was deep inside myself, floating in a sea of sensations. I was stretched around him. His cock was as deep as it could go; he filled me so tight he had to go at it very slowly, and then in one second, I let go.

He leaned over me, brushed my mouth with his lips. You were beautiful when you came, he said.

You're not bad at this yourself.

He smiled, pleased with himself.

When he got up, he patted his belly, covered with its soft dark down.

I had a check-up the other day. I put on ten pounds since last year. Can you tell?

I was amused by that sudden shift to intimate matters. You're still skinny, I said, although I *had* noticed he was growing a little pouch. In a few years, he would slip down the other side of middle age and grow a potbelly. Not that I would get to see it. Our affair would have long ended by then.

I remembered David at that age exactly. We were visiting friends upstate one summer, and I was sitting on the grass with Juliet. He was standing in profile, in shorts and bare-chested, and I could clearly see the outline of a belly. Late thirties and early forties are the age when a man can't get away with eating like a teenager anymore. Or when the beer catches up with him.

58

ANYTHING THAT HAS *my handwriting on it, you have to keep*, Louise texts me before coming to our Sunday evening dinner of Indian food and TV shows, while I fill recycling bags with her old drawings, schoolwork, photocopies, tests, reams of papers, and hefty SAT prep books.

I have started stripping the huge bulletin board hung in the hallway, covered with an accumulation of photos, medals won at gymnastics and track contests, birthday cards, cards drawn and collaged by artists friends, poems, concert tickets, political buttons, and snapshots of more than twenty years of life. I pull out the thumbtacks one by one, letting the photos and drawings and cards fall at my feet, curling up in the humidity, plundering the mausoleum of my past.

When Louise arrives, she finds me surrounded by a sea of photos. A thumbtack almost gets stuck in the sole of her sneaker, and she screams that high-pitched scream she let out when David told her—near the arch of Washington Square Park where we had arranged to meet him—that he wouldn't be living with us anymore, but with the *friend* Louise had met a couple of weeks earlier. That scream I still hear now when she is upset. A scream of panic. Her voice veering out of control, swelling with rage.

Mom! What are you doing with all the photos?

I kneel and open my arms, pick them up in big armfuls, carry them to a basket I have set on the table.

She stands above me, in judgment.

You're not going to throw the photos out, are you?

I am not throwing them out. I want to update the bulletin board.

I know you. You're going to throw them out.

No! I won't! I promise. I don't know what I am going to do. But we have plenty of photo albums. We'll put them in the albums. *You* can put them in the albums.

Where *are* the photo albums? Accusatory tone.

The vertigo again, riding a vague of guilt. I draw a blank.

I don't know.

Everything had gotten packed away, pushed in the back of the closets, photo albums, vinyl from the 60s and 70s left behind by David—Bob Dylan's *Highway 61 Revisited*, Cream, *Sgt. Pepper's Lonely Heart's Club Band*, The Doors, Jimi Hendrix Experience, and The Grateful Dead with their psychedelic swirls of album covers. And also the B-52's, the Ramones, the Sex Pistols, Bob Dylan's *Blood on the Tracks*, Led Zeppelin, and Tom Waits. The family videos, the old toys, the Barbies, the Rugrats, the My Little Ponys, the princess outfits, the pink tutus, the jeweled crowns, the lavender plastic mules, the multicolored crayons, the craft paper—detritus of an American girlhood—the half-toothless menorah with two bent candles stuck in it, the rugs hand woven by David's mom, the jars of instant Nescafé, the coupons clipped by David's father, the baby cubes hand-crocheted by David's sister, the keys to a defunct second-hand Chrysler LeBaron convertible David had briefly owned in the 90s, Enamored with that boat-sized classic American gondola of a car, he drove in winter with the top down, wearing a pimp fox fur coat, a fedora (already the fedora theme), and a pair of Ray-Ban aviators, he unloaded it after he failed to sell two screenplays in a row, the keys to all the cars, bicycles, lockers of our life together, now unrecognizable, unusable.

What hadn't been hastily pushed away had been thrown out in a hurry or sent to the Salvation Army like after someone died.

Don't keep all those books on your side table, Wang Jing had admonished, eyeing the piles of novels and poetry crowded around my reading lamp.

I protested: I am a reader. I need to read before going to sleep.

She shook her head.

Books speak, she said, they whisper. They get into your dreams. They won't let your mind rest at night.

Which was, of course, exactly what I had always craved, the murmuring of stories, the words filling my head, my soul. How empty would I feel without them?

Obedient, I carried them by the armful and slipped them haphazardly on my bookshelves. There was never enough time to organize, let alone alphabetize. Books climbed up the walls between the brick walls in true New York loft fashion.

But books are not the only ones that talk and whisper and lurk in the dark.

So where *are* they, *mom*? You don't even know where the albums are, *do you?*

Sometimes Louise takes on her dad's tone. That angry and scornful edge that had become permanent in our last couple of years—the scorn of the man who feels trapped.

Her eyes bore into me like a judge before she brings her gavel down.

I was supposed to be the guardian of the past, of the family life. Obviously, I failed. I tried to be the mother I didn't have. And now, suddenly, I want no part of it. I know I've tossed a stone in the middle of the memory lake. I've committed a sacrilege.

On the bulletin board, the hundreds of pinholes left from the thumbtacks form an abstract pattern, the scarification of our lives.

Scorched earth policy. Crops burnt to the roots. Nothing can grow back for years.

Okay, let's order food, Louise says, pivoting, her voice pinched, walking away from the carnage. Still playing the father's role. Law and order. And I realize to my astonishment that I've continued to play the same role with Louise as I did with David: on the defensive, apologetic for pursuing my career, for my ambition, for taking too much space, for not being on top of the food shopping and cooking situation, for being distracted, head in the clouds. For not being a good mother, a good wife. Relationships fall apart in the gap between your idea of yourself and the idea your partner has of you.

While we wait for the food to be delivered, Louise is bundled into the throw blanket, compulsively checking her phone. She's worried her boyfriend is not texting her as often as he used to. The wind rattles the windows. Snowstorm is announced for the night. She'll sleep here and go straight to work tomorrow.

Pull away a little, I say. Give him some space.

Louise is outraged. She doesn't want to play games. She just wants to know what's going on. I give her bad advice. She needs a mom who gives her more conventional, normal advice. And what is that? Louise, who, among other features—dark almond shaped eyes, lovely lips and delicate nose—has inherited her grandmother's fiery eyes and temper, lashes out:

You. You screw up everything with men. Look at you now. Alone.

I have my work, I say. My writing. You and Juliet. Vivian. And what's this about me being "alone." What's wrong with that? I thought you were a feminist.

She gets up angrily, starts clearing the dishes. When she comes back, she picks up my hand, which is significantly more wrinkled than my face (I always forget to lather sunscreen on it) and is dotted with what we used to call liver spots although personally I prefer to think of them as large freckles. She gently runs a finger across the texture of the skin and looks at me with a sad face. I think it means: mom, you're not so young anymore. Louise's big fear is to have to take care of me when I'm old and the idea of that burden is terrifying to her. But perhaps that's a reductive interpretation. Louise loves me, I think, deep down, and she's keenly observant of every detail and nuances. She would have made a good writer if she hadn't decided to become an actress.

59

IN A FIT of repulsion, I attack the food closet. For too long, now, I've been living at the edge of my life, on top of my past, still festering, still silently roaming in the shadows. Boxes and cans way past their expiration dates huddle at the back of the pantry, perhaps even dating back from before David's exit. They instantly become unbearable to keep, to even look at. I take a large garbage bag and fill it in a kind frenzy with rice and quinoa and mysterious bags of flour or cornmeal, even though I practically never bake. I dump the cans and the cardboard boxes and the plastic bottles and take the garbage bag to the street.

Two days later a series of close-ups of the inside of my trash bag pop up in my inbox. *WHO DUMPED THIS?* In the subject line. The email is from the person in charge of garbage and recycling in my coop. There's just one line of text: *We got a $200 FINE from the sanitation department. WHO IS RESPONSIBLE?*

My cheeks flush in shame. Not just because I flouted the rules of recycling, but for having my old trash exposed to my neighbors in revealing close-ups. Worse than dirty laundry.

It was me, I answer, I'll pay the fine. I go down to the basement where the incriminating bag has been stored, kneel in front of it as penance, and sort it out.

For years, old VHS and audiocassettes have been stacked in a bookcase along one living room wall. Until Jonah mentioned them, I was blind to them. And now the scales have fallen off my eyes and they look like an abomination. The shelves sagging under the weights of cassettes untouched for more than a decade, stacked two or three rows deep, gathering dust, crushing me.

Louise loved the old school tapes of her first years, the family scenes David religiously captured on video and sent copies of to his parents in Boca. When he left, he took his camera with him. After that, he recorded another family. And it didn't occur to me to pick up the mantle of the parent who videotaped, who photographed, who documented the family life. So, after David was gone, which was before the advent of the smartphone, there would be no more family scenes recorded for posterity, and Louise couldn't see herself growing up anymore.

To preserve these early videos, I had them transferred to digital files.

Everything else could go.

The next weekend, Louise and I get huge black plastic bags and stuff them with armful of cassettes. We fill out at least ten thirty-gallon trash bags. These bags are filled with alien things, made of plastic and recording tape, so obsolete neither the garbage nor the sanitation truck would accept them. The only solution is the public trashcan at the street corner. That is forbidden as well, but what other option do we have? So we each carry one huge black bag on our shoulders at dusk. Louise goes back for a second one while I carry mine as surreptitiously as possible when you are carrying a 30 gallon bag full to the hilt and dump it at the corner. When it's all done, I tell a neighbor about it, and the neighbor says: don't you know that it's a $1000 fine if you're caught dumping things in the corner trash bin?

How do you get rid of the past then?

60

AT THE BEGINNING of Tarkovsky's *The Mirror*, a young woman is sitting on a fence in the countryside, facing a vast expanse of green field. It is a beautiful summer day. A man walks up to her looking for directions. They start to talk, and he lingers. She dodges his questions, but you can tell she's interested. He sits down on the fence by her side, and the fence collapses under them. The camera cuts away, and we see two little kids in a hammock. Perhaps the husband is gone. We don't know what will happen, if the man and the woman will get involved. The man is a gypsy, a musician, a poet, a cowboy, he's a man with a nebulous mission, more at ease in his own head than in the world of brick and mortar. This is the kind of man I've always been attracted to.

It stands to reason if your father disappears before you were born, you develop all kinds of unconscious dreams about men. Men are the most compelling when they vanish, when they live offstage, when their life barely intersects with yours, when their absence is a powerful engine of fantasy. They showed me a photo of my father when I was about eight. A young man with his blond hair slicked back, a white shirt open at the neck and his shirtsleeves rolled up as if he was about to go boating or to a picnic. I stared at the photo in panic without touching it. I didn't want to put a face on a ghost.

The only memory I have of my mother with a man goes so far back in my childhood I sometimes think I made it up. There are just a few scattered images: a little girl alone in the yard of a farmhouse, surrounded by puddles and beaten earth, scared, looking for a bracelet she has lost. It's a thin, gold, diamond-shaped chain encrusted with tiny turquoise beads inlaid at the center of each diamond. How far back can one remember? Three years old maybe? I'm alone in the yard, crying, looking for my beloved bracelet. Suddenly, the front door of the house opens and a tall, burly man comes out with my mother. They seem annoyed. They look around and finally the man, leaning forward, picks the bracelet out of a puddle and hands it to me.

One summer day, I took Vadik to a guinguette, one of these old school riverside dancing restaurants along the Marne River, east of Paris, which were popular around 1900 and have kept their quaint charm. Before dinner we took a walk on the pathway along the river, and a town sign emerged from the thicket of trees. A classic French white enamel sign framed with a thin red stripe, the name of the town in black block letters. *CHAMPIGNY*. I stopped short. The name had a sickening familiarity, emerging from a deep fog, a nightmare suddenly come to life. My throat was dry.

I used to imagine my mother as an Amazon. She worked as a fashion designer's assistant and took August off to travel on her own. She brought me back exotic presents: a local costume from Zagreb; silver bracelets from Marrakesh; and singles of Serbian folk music to play on my little orange record player while we danced under the disapproving eyes of my grandmother. My mother was always coming and going as far as I could remember. Disappearing for days in a fit of anger. Leaving to study medicine at the University of Lyon and coming back after two years, no degree in hand. She was gone. Weekends, evenings. Summers. Sometimes she showed up at dinner. Sometimes not. Or late at night. She was a whirlwind, a tornado. Loud laughs. Low-cut blouses. The clack of high heels. Doors banging. Perfume and cigarette smoke trailing behind her. One day years later, after her death, my godfather told me my mother had lived with a man in Champigny when I was little. He had a farm. He was violent. I had gone to preschool there for a semester. My grandparents were so worried they came to get me and refused to let me go back. I remembered none of that. Only the terror of having lost my bracelet. I told Vadik the story of the bracelet. That's where I lost it. Here. He squeezed my hand tight.

When you are in your thirties and forties, you think things will fall into place when you're older, when the choices you've made somehow coalesce into one clear road of maturity and wisdom. The right companion, the right creative way, serenity achieved.

But the thing about getting older is that you see life from a different perspective. You see its outlines—the beginning and the end—like when you are on a ship in the middle of the ocean, and you're surrounded by the curvature of the earth. It's unsettling, as if you were already half out of your life yet still in the thick of it at the same time.

At my age, my mother was roaming the world, my grandmother had eight grandchildren, a husband of forty years, a big, comfortable villa, and a summer home. She had short gray hair rinsed blue and wore flowered housedresses. Was she happy? She had achieved what society expected of her. And there was probably a kind of happiness or contentment of a life lived according to the rules.

On the phone, Lena asks me, "Will we ever be happy again?" I know what she means. Falling in love with "The One." Embarking into a blissful romance. My French friends mention, in passing, how so and so just met someone at age sixty-eight, or seventy-one. They're madly in love, won't leave the bedroom. How they are going off to Capri, to Ibiza. I don't say anything.

I see myself in my writing studio, flooded with light, in the thick of a novel, interrupted with occasional visits by a young, passionate lover.

61

THE FENG SHUI uncluttering and rearranging is a double-edged sword. Corners are dusted off, the eye can travel from one end of a room to another. Ghosts recede. Perhaps even disintegrate in the dust. I marvel at the space newly created. Like an empty stage awaiting a new play.

I have finished a rough first draft of my screenplay that seems solid. I could do a private table reading of a few scenes and ask Louise to read the daughter's part. Invite a group of writers and filmmakers as an audience, and the room would be alive again. If only I could ask Jonah to come and play the piano, do a bit of improv. But he'd never cross that line. And I wouldn't dare ask him.

At first Louise is skeptical. She has only read two of my books, the novel that takes place in a little French island off the Mediterranean coast, where the lovers find a body in the eucalyptus forest, and my memoir about meeting my father. I am concerned Louise might read the screenplay as the symbolic murder of her father. She is a tough critic. But when she emerges, the script rolled in her hands, she seems excited.

In the scenes that I want to try out, the daughter has just found out she's pregnant, and she tells her mom that she wants to keep the baby. The boyfriend is there too, and he's overwhelmed by the situation. Both he and the mom would be much relieved if the daughter did the right thing in their mind, which is to get an abortion. Meanwhile, they just found out the father is having an affair, and the whole family is on the brink of collapse.

62

I HAVE INVITED a dozen friends, writers, and filmmakers. Lena is there, of course, and Annie, the young woman from the writing group, who's become a friend—we regularly meet at the little café to discuss writing and publishing—and Kirsty and Mark, my favorite couple. Kirsty and Mark are both in their mid-fifties. I met them when their daughter and Louise were both in kindergarten together, and we've remained friends ever since, as they moved to LA, then to Paris, and back to New York. She's Scottish and designs furniture, a lovely, vivacious redhead, and he's American, a tech guy.

We've spent vacations and weekends together. They are great friends, smart and fun, and still very much together after twenty-five years, even though they'd each had an affair or two along the way. I admire the way they've gotten over the infidelities and managed to keep their independence and their physical and intellectual complicity at the same time and they seem still genuinely fond of each other. I hang out with both of them, together or separately—at a concert with Mark, or a dinner date with Kirsty. Their couple doesn't feel like a fortress but like a welcoming island. Not something that David and I ever tried. Perhaps, if we had, things would have turned out differently.

We are all sitting around the living room area, some on the floor, some on the couch and chairs, in the middle of the dramatic scene, as the mom is aiming her revolver with both fists at her ex-husband, when the buzzer rings. We all laugh.

Saved by the bell!

It's Alan, just back from a show in Barcelona. He puts his suitcase down and joins us to listen to the last scene. Then we grab beers from the fridge and uncork bottles of wine and eat the salads Louise and I have prepared.

Lena is gushing about Louise's interpretation. I concur.

What did you think, Louise? You were good.

Oh please. You're not objective. To be honest, I think you should tweak the daughter's dialogue. It feels kind of… sentimental? Or too wordy? But the scene worked.

Louise's approval is like an unexpected gift, deposited at my feet. A tiny opening of the door she keeps so tightly closed between us. This is all thanks to the feng shui, I think. Wang Jing was right about the uncluttering.

After everyone left and I was dozing off in bed, I heard the door to my room open and a faint shuffle. I thought it was Kiki-the-cat. I always left the door cracked open for her. But the body that alighted by my side was way heavier than the cat's little body. Alan had found his way under the comforter and pressed himself against me.

What are you doing?

What?

You're drunk.

Nah.

There's something about having been with someone before that opens the door to a certain casualness of rapport, although when David had tossed me on the couch the evening he had come to babysit Louise, the break was so deep, so irrevocable that I had lost all desire. But there was always an undercurrent of flirtation between Alan and me.

What about Maria?

He kissed me sloppily to shut me up and made his way down my belly.

I didn't resist. It was surprisingly delicious. The pent-up frustration with Jonah caused by his dance of one step forward and two backward needed an outlet. In fact, it was a sweet revenge, like with Frederic, the German guitarist. It was obviously a private revenge since Jonah would never know about it. But it felt good and that was all that mattered.

The next morning when I woke up, I was alone in bed and wondered if it had been a dream. I found Alan in the kitchen, already up since the crack of dawn from jet lag, preparing coffee, the rich smell wafting like a promise of blissful domesticity.

What about Maria, I said again, sitting down in front of the cup he had filled.

I think she's going back to her husband.

What? Are you serious?

To be honest, I don't know. Not sure I care at this point.

I looked at him without saying anything. He held my gaze.

What's with *Jazzman*?

In the past it might have been a good ending for a novel. These two, who lived well together, two artists understanding each other, good companions, long discussions late into the nights. The protagonist, finally coming back to her senses after a foolish love affair, makes the reasonable choice. But such is the vagary of life that it doesn't always work that way. Alan drank too much, he loved unstable women, he had an on and off girlfriend. He wasn't reasonable. Although neither was I, apparently. So maybe we were right for each other for that very reason. Fleetingly I wondered if I was wrong about that relationship, which I always thought was better as friendship than as love. Vadik had been the closest to a true companion since David. We had maintained our long-distance relationship for almost six years. When the three of us, Louise, Vadik, and I, had gone cross-country skiing near my godfather's home in the Valais, there had briefly been a glimmer of a possible family.

He's coming around again, I said.

Still not tired of it?

Was there a hint of hope in Alan's question?

I have a rule of thumb: I take the pain as long as there's enough pleasure to outweigh the pain. And then I'm done.

It's called the law of diminishing returns.

63

A FEW DAYS later, I was eating with Lena and Alan at a little Mexican taco place in Nolita. We were all sitting at the counter in a row, passing guacamole and tortilla chips back and forth while waiting for our fish tacos. Alan had ordered Dos Equis for everyone.

Have you ever thought of marrying a rich financier who could take care of you? Lena asked. You'd be free to write and you wouldn't have money pressure anymore.

Don't listen to her, Alan said. She doesn't believe a word of it, and she would never have done it.

Lena giggled.

Actually, I've been meeting a slew of them, she continued.

Who? Financiers? On the dating site?

Yup. I am treating it as anthropology.

Lena's last few dates were with men in their sixties. One wore a testosterone patch; the other one popped Viagra like candy. In the past, she figured, if those men had been married for thirty or forty years, they may have just let their sexuality dwindle while they played golf and their wives shopped. Unless of course they took a mistress. But now their wives are leaving them or they're widowers, and the pressure is on to perform, to keep up with the young and not so young women they want to date. Most single women in New York, whatever their age, expect a certain level of performance from men.

Oh God, I chuckled. Maybe it's worse for them than for us?

I exchanged a complicit glance with Alan. He hadn't hit sixty yet. He smiled vaguely but seemed to want to distance himself.

When he had crawled into my bed the night after the reading of the screenplay, he certainly hadn't needed a testosterone patch. Where do they put these patches anyway?

Would my rich financier come equipped with a testosterone patch? Or perhaps finance attracts exceptionally virile alpha males who remain priapic, no matter their age. They say that for some women, money is an aphrodisiac. But wouldn't it be more of an aphrodisiac if you made the money yourself? Better a young, fickle lover or no man at all, I thought.

We ordered more beer. The conversation was drifting into a weird place.

We were trying to reconcile the impossible conundrum of our generation: how to remain sexual and relevant and vibrant as you get older and break the old stereotypes and at the same time deal creatively with the inevitable changes. Lena, who had gotten white hair in her thirties, now had a glorious mane of silver, which she twisted in a messy bun on top of her head. Alan had started to grow a salt and pepper beard and mustache, and his short, spiky hair still had a punk flavor. At times, when I was tired of the constant upkeep which I did myself at home, I was tempted to let my hair go white and wild. I did yoga every day, and my body was still lean and tight, even though the oval of my face was getting soft, the telltale sign of aging, but I took it in stride.

As a generation, we had broken the old rules. Put everything out in the open. Open the closet, expose the dirty laundry, everything up for grabs, every belief challenged, marriage, gender, relationships, like a bucket of confetti tossed up in the air. And our children had pushed it several steps farther. There was no new system, but a continual reinvention. God was gone, replaced by yoga and mindfulness. Nobody wanted to go back to the old ways. But everybody was groping for new ways. On Instagram, some women in their sixties and seventies seemed to have found the answer: running on the beach in Malibu or Venice Beach, with their tan, gazelle legs, their long white manes floating in the wind. The new amazons. On her feed, Lena was often contacted by young men whose presence online (considering the paltry number of followers they had) seemed only designed to hit on women.

I put my hand over my glass when Alan offered to order more beer. Lena had already switched to water. He would drink the last bottle by himself.

Maybe we should quit while we're ahead, I said.

Lena pulled out her phone to check her messages and shook her head.

You don't mean it.

I don't know. Truly. I mean… I don't know.

Alan, who was sitting between us, dropped his hand on my thigh.

There was a silence. Lena was typing a text on her phone.

One of your testosterone-challenged suitors?

Ha! No. Sorry. I have to meet with a student tomorrow.

Oh well, we'll always have our work, I said, lifting Alan's hand off my thigh. Alone in a garret or in a ramshackle cabin somewhere in the country, typing or painting away or playing music until our fingers fall off.

We burst out into laughter. We were tossing jokes at life as if brandishing crosses or heads of garlic to force back vampires.

Lena signaled to the waiter and we each dropped our card in the tray.

We won't be alone, I said. We'll have each other. Right?

Nobody laughed at that. It was cutting it too close to the bone.

Alan slid his arm around my shoulders.

I'll walk you back.

Thanks. But you're living at my place right now, so that doesn't count.

On the way out, we bumped into Kirsty and Mark, who had just had dinner in the neighborhood and were on their way to the R train. I loved it when New York turned into a village, and you ran into your friends unexpectedly.

They're my role models as a couple, I told Alan, half joking, afterward.

They've both had affairs, you know, Alan said.

I know.

The wind picked up on Houston Street straight from the East River when we emerged from the side street. How deserted and seedy that bit used to be when you passed Ludlow, walking east. How grimy, how derelict, how devastated the whole neighborhood used to be, abandoned or burnt down, left for dead and yet vibrant with life, wildflowers pushing through the cracks, empty lots reclaimed as gardens. And now condos loomed tall between organic markets, gourmet *gelateria* and retro diners, while NYU students tottered around hammered at one a.m. without fear of getting mugged. Only the rats didn't get the memo, their continued presence unseemly, obscene, in the gentrified neighborhood. Or maybe they just added the requisite touch of grittiness.

In the apartment, Alan followed me to my bedroom without missing a beat.

No, I said, leaning on the doorjamb. The other night was good, but not to be continued.

Because of *Jazzman*?

No. It just doesn't feel right. We're friends. Right?

Yes, of course. But…

I know… But. No. We wouldn't be a good couple.

Who's talking about being a couple?

I went up to him, kissed him on the mouth, and gently pushed him out.

He was in the kitchen the next morning as though nothing had happened. The pungent scent of fresh Brazilian coffee, the steaming mugs, the sublime taste of toasted peasant bread, butter, and marmalade. The first conversation of the day about art and politics. Things were back to where I wanted them.

After breakfast, Alan showed up in the kitchen, carrying a load of wet clothes.

Hey, are you aware that your dryer's on the blink?

The idea of a broken dryer made me sick. Appliances were the bane of my existence. Always conking out unexpectedly and then life had to be turned upside down, and none of them ever cost less than $1000, it never failed, and the new one always looked more or less like the exact replica of the previous one.

I found Alan, a few minutes later, squatting in front of the dryer examining the door mechanism. It was at least twenty years old. I remembered getting it when Louise was still in diapers. I'd already been googling clothes dryers and grabbed the tape measure to check the dimensions.

Alan stood up, holding a tiny gadget between his thumb and forefinger with a double prong sticking out.

I think I found your problem. This little thingy here is broken. That's what secures the door. If I hold the door closed with my hand, it works perfectly. See?

He put his wet clothes back in the dryer and wedged the door shut with a chair. The familiar rumbling came on.

He placed the gadget on the kitchen counter.

You ought to be able to get a piece like that in a company that sells appliance parts. Snap it into the door, and it'll be good as new.

Wow! You're right.

Maybe, come to think of it, what I missed most about life with a man—besides regular sex, that is—was that technically minded way of figuring things out, good with tools, adept at fixing things, figuring what peg fits into what hole in a flash, repairing a car carburetor—at least, most of the men I'd been with had been like that. François, David, even Vadik had fixed the carburetor when his old Land Rover had broken down on the way to the Matterhorn. Of course, plenty of women could do it too, but, sadly, I wasn't one of them.

Once I'd had a friend from Paris who had fixed my long-leaking toilet flush. In exchange, I had sewn buttons on a coat he had bought at a flea market in Brooklyn. I thought we'd make a good team.

Sure enough, five minutes later I had spotted the little gizmo online for eight dollars.

That's amazing, I said. I'm *so* going to miss you when you leave.

64

ONE LATE AFTERNOON, as I had gone out to run some errands, I stepped into a crack in the sidewalk on my way back home and my ankle gave way. For an instant there was a suspension of all feeling and strength in my left foot, but when I regained my balance and tried to step on it, there was an acute pain. I hobbled to the nearest bench, the very bench on which Jonah was sitting almost a year ago, restringing a guitar, when I had run into him. I removed my boot and slipped a finger into my sock to feel the ankle. From where I was sitting, I had a good view of the avenue where he rode up on his bicycle or walked to pick up his car. It was very close to the time he usually left the studio. How stupid of me to have concocted this outing—getting cash at the bank, which I could have easily done the next day—while a fierce wind blew all the way from the East River, and now my hair was flying this way and that like a madwoman and I had one foot half naked. What if he suddenly appeared between the desolate elms? In French we have a saying: *marcher à côté de ses pompes*. It means to walk besides one's shoes, your head in the clouds, your feet blind. It had taken almost a whole year for my knee to heal, and now I was injuring myself again.

I limped back home to ice my ankle, but I was so frustrated, so angry at myself that, to loosen up the cold pack I kept in the freezer, I banged it against the edge of the glass coffee table and broke the glass. I burst into tears. I knew I was acting like a child, like a crazy woman, that I had brought it all upon herself. If I went down that road, I would end up like the piano teacher in

Haneke's movie. The writing group would be thrilled. I had to get a grip.

Three days later, I got a call from my accountant's assistant announcing I had to pay $8000 in taxes to the IRS. How was that possible? I'd have to dip into my savings. I knew I had made quite a bit more money last year translating the website of the American designer. But in this city, money slips through your fingers if you don't watch it like a hawk. I hadn't put money aside for the taxes. I usually got a refund. Hoping there was an error, I tried to speak to my accountant, but couldn't get him on the phone. He was busy preparing returns and ignored the messages I left with his assistant.

Why did I neglect the wealth and abundance corner and the health corner, to focus on the relationship corner? So much for setting my priorities straight. Life is about balancing. I literally couldn't stand on my own two feet. I put one foot on the edge of a broken piece of sidewalk, and my ankle collapses. And spraining my ankle in the off chance of running into Jonah was the sign that I was losing control over my life.

I had to finish the screenplay. It was the only way I could get my career moving forward again. The read-through had been positive, but I still had a lot of work to do.

65

I HAD BEEN writing all afternoon. I could feel the energy of the scenes carrying me over. When I was writing and it was going well, everything else fell away. I was in the flow. Life was good. So when his text popped up, it threw me off. I stared at it, debating my options. What if I disappeared like he did, with a flip of my tail?

Hey Eve. Should we meet up soon?

Like that, out of the blue. As if an invisible thread kept us connected, even after weeks of absence.

I counted the months since we first met. A year and a half. It was weird to even think of the time that had passed, since we didn't see each other regularly between these long gaps. Our affair existed in another time—a parallel time, online time. Not real life time. It was that dream-like quality that was so seductive.

Are you free tonight?

He had a meeting in Manhattan. Wasn't sure at what time it would end. An hour later, he cancelled. His car had been towed.

185 bucks. Those fuckers!

He texted me back the next morning to apologize and offered to send me an Uber to make up for last night. He was working at home. I didn't even hesitate. Ten minutes later, we were crossing the Williamsburg Bridge.

It was a jolt to be at his place for the first time—the tangible reality of it.

Sorry. It's a bit messy. Just got back from traveling. Haven't had time to clean up.

But it wasn't. Not messy, just lived in. There was a good, focused vibe of someone who kept his life simple, down to the essential. I knew he had moved there soon after 9/11. It was rent stabilized. He couldn't believe his luck.

He helped me out of my jacket, my bag, kneeled to unbuckle my shoes.

Here you are, he said, gesturing ironically across the one room. Want to visit?

It was an old railroad apartment that had been opened. The kitchen at one end, a living space with a couch at the other, his workspace and unmade bed in the middle. His ten guitars, his keyboard, his desktop computer. A laptop on the kitchen table, tiny bathroom on the side. The windows full of plants—the very plants I had seen on his web site photos—small succulents, orchids, a luxurious rubber plant. A fig tree.

My father gave me the orchids when I first moved in, he said when I examined them.

They looked like miniature acrobats floating in tiny wooden baskets in front of the window. Did I know that orchids were air plants? I didn't know. One flower was peaking, a deep purple streaked with pale yellow, both delicate and sumptuous.

There was a newspaper clipping held by a magnet on the fridge. A black and white picture of a doctor, wearing a white coat over a turtleneck and thin wire-rimmed glasses, sitting at his desk with a plaque in Hebrew. An advertisement for a hospital in Tel Aviv. The same picture I had seen online.

Is that your father?

Yeah.

He doesn't look like you at all.

I don't see him very much.

Because he lives in Tel Aviv?

We didn't live with him. He left my mother when I was five. Went to live with another woman in Israel. He had grown up there and gone to college, so it was like going home, I guess. But anyway. I didn't grow up with him.

You were the same age as Louise when my ex left me. And then he had a baby right away.

My dad too. Jonah said.

What?? Like you?

He nodded.

But that's... that's... grotesque. Cruel. Why?

He shrugged.

His wife liked the name, I guess.

That upset me. Imagine David having a daughter and naming her Louise.

And he's a psychiatrist?

I know, right? I guess he wanted to please her.

If I had been your mom, I'd have been pissed.

I think she was.

What about you?

We didn't see them very much. It doesn't matter now.

We were still awkwardly standing by the fridge. He looked away.

I didn't know what to say. It seemed intrusive to force his intimacy. The door that had cracked open the last few months was closing again.

But you didn't come to talk about my father.

We went to the couch. He pointed to the mirror across from it, on the floor, leaning against an unused fireplace.

See, I have a mirror too.

Did he always have it positioned that way? For Emma? For the girls who came to visit? Or had he placed it for me—for us? I thought of the way he had put the stool in front of the mirror in the recording studio when I had gone there.

He leaned toward the table where I had placed my glasses and slipped them on my face.

From where we were half-sitting, half-lying down, the mirror framed us exactly—his back and my legs laced around his neck, in the black stockings that he would rip at the crotch, my shirt partially unbuttoned. A perfect erotic shot.

Afterward, I sat up and pulled back a little to look at him, his sensuous mouth, his beard, his thick hair.

What was age? I felt the same—almost—as I did thirty years ago when I had met David, that frigid January first in the Upper East Side. Yet there's no denying the thickness of time. That's what attracts him, I thought, that mystery. That world of experience in me that he cannot grasp. Separating us like an ocean.

What? He searched my eyes. For a second, we crossed the gap and there it was—a real closeness.

I really like you, he said. You're awesome.

He seemed so chill. But underneath his cool, there was that tension coiled tight, that wall of protection.

After we made love, I got dressed and dawdled, stood by the keyboard.

Do you compose on it?

Yes. I play too. I am playing Bach right now.

Bach. There was so much I didn't know about him. And he knew even less about me. He had only tiptoed into my life. It was both terribly sexy and unsettling, as though we just stood at each other's edge, not daring to enter.

I looked at the books scattered on the shelf behind his bed—W.G. Sebald (I thought of *Mack The Knife*, the Sebald scholar in Edinburg, and of my own Sebald collection), Murakami, Peter Matthiessen, Dostoïevsky's *Brothers Karamazov*.

We're reading the same books.

I only have a few now. When I like a book, I give it away.

He was looking at me, amused, back in his chino pants, his shirtsleeves rolled up as if ready for a day of hard labor. His mood had changed. The keyboard was waiting, Bach was waiting, his ten guitars in their black cases were stomping their feet.

I gotta get back to work. Big rehearsal tonight.

Maybe he was already regretting I had come to see him, invading his space, getting closer to him. Already regretting that weakness he'd had, that nuclear, explosive desire men have that has to be satisfied in the moment, and then afterward, this urge to deny the moment. Feeling guilty to have led me on. Ashamed to have given in to his impulse. Amazed to see that I was still there, lingering. Picking up a book, threatening to start a conversation, a literary conversation of all things, inquisitively leaning over the keyboard as if pushing my foot in the door, asking for a glass of water when he was finishing a bottle of orange juice and tossing it in the garbage without offering me any, because in his mind I was already gone, erased. No memory of what we had just done in front of the mirror, when he collapsed into my arms, and that moment of tenderness, Look at me, I want to see you come, his fingers gently pushing the hair from my face.

I had wanted so badly to go to his place in the early days.

A flash of anger burnt into my chest. It was too late to play that game. I couldn't give him another chance, wait for him to come around again. I was a fool to think he could overcome his fears and misgivings. Maybe it was about Emma, his soon-to-be ex-wife. The moments we had shared in Montauk and our nights at my place were moments of weakness, not of love.

He was rinsing his glass under the tap, and turned sharply toward me with that smile he had to know was irresistible to women, and certainly to me, his elbows leaning against the sink.

What's the matter?

Without a word, I kneeled to buckle my shoes. Slipped on my jacket.

Eve?

I shook my head. What was the point? Throw a scene? Leave in a huff? His ironic detachment had put us back where he wanted. In control. He had closed the door. Did he really not understand? Did he deny what had happened between us? Would he bury it as a hot memory and revisit it from time to time when he would be married to another woman, and then later when the marriage floundered?

I have to go.

Do you want me to call a car? Let me walk down with you.

It's okay. I'm good.

I walked toward the L in the early spring sun. My ankle was still wobbly, but I barely felt it. I was floating along the streets of Bushwick and Williamsburg, past industrial buildings and car muffler shops, merging into the hipster crowd, past the trendy cafés and restaurants, past the boutiques full of overpriced knick-knacks and clothes made in Brooklyn, the new destination of world cool, rushing toward the subway, the glow of our connection unraveling into shreds.

Back in Manhattan, I walked through the park, where the new buds created a halo of pale green against the hard blue sky. I wanted to feel the ground under my feet, walk it out. Students were lying on the lawn in the sun, half-undressed, craving the first heat of the year. I called Lena.

It's over, I said.

What happened?

I started to walk across the roundabout, toward the huge elm, then traced my steps back. Back and forth. Back and forth.

Nothing. He's making me feel so *alive.* Like I used to feel with David. I can't go on. He's too close to what I want. But I can't have him.

Nobody can *have* anybody.

At least, she spared me. She didn't say she knew it all along. Or it was doomed from the start.

That evening, as I was pulling down my window shade, one of the two red hearts I had placed on the windowsill fell down and broke into tiny pieces.

66

LOVERBABE, 48 – Can I show you my cock you mind Maybe you'll like

Crazy4Love, 46 – You're obviously very artistic, I'd love to meet you and your mind (Must be amazing in there)

PassingthroughNY, 61 – You sound marvelous. Sven from Copenhagen.

IMarseille, 42 – Un baiser sur le genou

B my lover.

Would you like to go out with a young stud like me?

Hey sexy!

I am a G-d-fearing man and find you irresistibly attractive.

Hey, I'm Jason. You're beautiful. Are you a banana? Because you are so A-peeling.

I'm Alex!

Hi, I'm John. Bonjour pretty lady.

John12tiger, 54 – Hello beautiful woman, how are you doing?

I read the messages that had accumulated in the last few weeks. Meaningless, trashy pickup lines. I felt a wave of vertigo, the blood leaving my chest, my stomach heaving.

In one click, I deactivated my profile.

67

I WAS AT Juliet's home in Jacksonville, the two of us having breakfast on the deck while Vivian played quietly at our feet, when I got a missed call from an unknown number. When I picked up the voicemail, I instantly recognized the rolled "r", the Slavic accent.

Salut chérie, C'est Vadim.

Not Vadik, his nickname, but his formal name, Vadim, that he never used back when we were together. He always spoke French with me when he wanted to be intimate, and his Russian accent sounded more exotic, softer in French. He was in Moscow, heading to New York in a few weeks. He wanted to see me.

What? Who was it? asked Juliet, looking up from the blanket where she was sitting with Vivian. Like Louise, she was immediately alerted to any change of tone or vibe from me, like the wind suddenly blowing from a different direction or a cloud passing over the sun, although she was calmer about my subtle changes of moods than Louise, who had inherited my hair trigger tendency to alarm.

Vadik.

Years ago he would call me from Moscow, from Geneva, from Nairobi, from Islamabad, from Tashkent, from Samarqand, from Vienna, all in that same soft voice. He would switch to Russian, *Milaya moya*—My honey—melting words at the time. And the combination of these exotic places and his accent was irresistible to me. How long had it been? Six years? Seven? After so long, his voice sounded intact but also strangely disembodied, like a bee preserved in amber. Perhaps that's what happened with ex-lovers.

Even now, when I heard David's voice, I had a visceral reaction, although it stirred a mix of unpleasant images like when you plunge a stick in the bottom of a riverbed and the muck comes up, muddying the surface of the water.

More messages followed. I always missed his calls. When we finally spoke, he sounded excited, almost giddy, and for a brief moment, I felt the old excitement. What do you want me to bring you back from Moscow? How about a bottle of vodka? Standard, the brand he always bought in Geneva. He called me again when I was back in the city. I am excited to see you, he said. But each phone call eroded a tiny bit of my excitement and edged me toward the present, stripping the past of its aura. He had even called a couple of times without leaving a message. I recognized the phone number. The insistence made me feel suffocated. It reminded me how he got jealous when I once flew straight to Paris instead of meeting him in Geneva, how he hated when I alluded to David, even in passing. But when he called again to confirm our date, he sounded upbeat and relaxed.

We had met through a mutual Russian friend who arranged a dinner for the two of us. When I saw his extraordinary blue eyes, his beautiful face with the high cheekbones, the subtle wit of his comments about American politics and the way he looked at me, I was ready to embark on a Russian romance. He worked as an economist for the UN in Geneva and was supposed to be transferred to New York, where he had lived and worked in the past, although his transfer didn't happen. His English and his French were flawless, except for the accent that charmed me. It was such a change from insular America, a man who was not only a world traveler—a citizen of the world, as he called himself ironically—but was at ease in many languages and cultures.

I picked the restaurant. A classic French bistro in the West village, elegant but not trendy. Low key. Not the raucous sound level favored by New York restaurateurs. He was waiting for me at the door, smoking a cigarette.

I see him from the back. Baseball cap, tan jacket, slacks. In my memory he has longer hair, jeans, and a black jacket. A bandana, even, in the pictures taken in the south of France, and Ray-Bans, a Johnny Depp vibe. Tonight he looks like a midlevel civil servant.

He squashes his cigarette with his heel and gallantly holds the door for me. He has just had a business meeting, he says, to explain his clothes. We sit across from each other at the table. White linen. Old school stem glasses for the wine. Napkins elegantly folded in the glasses. Soft, rosy lighting. Black and white photos of New York City then and now. I look for him in his face, his eyes, which seem gray tonight, not the aquamarine blue that I remember, and that any girl would have killed for. Eyes do not change color like hair, so it must be the lighting. His beautiful aquiline nose, his well-formed lips. I can't find him. He's flattened, gray.

It's me, I am convinced. My gaze. The way I look at him. Objectively he hasn't changed that much. The light is soft, the atmosphere is subdued, the waiters unobtrusive. He wants red meat and red wine. I suggest a wine from the Loire Valley and order a rack of lamb. Even though I am more of a vegetarian now. But the occasion seems to call for meat. There's a lot to catch up on. He was in Lebanon. Then in South Sudan. Lebanon was better, better food, better entertainment. He laughs. Sudan is a compound, cut off from the rest of the country. And no alcohol!

But his laugh is a little sad. His news is not good. His mother had a stroke, and he spent the better part of last year taking care of her in Moscow, setting her up with a nurse, so she could have as much as a normal life as possible. And now he was thinking of retiring in Bali.

I recently met an Irish journalist whose dream is to retire in Bali. The girls are very young and beautiful, the beaches blindingly white, the sea the same aquamarine as Vadik's eyes, the weather paradisiac year-round—provided no tsunami hits you while you sip on a Bali Hai at dusk sprawled on the silky sand, your toes gently licked by the warm water, your potbelly expanding in the setting sun.

Unless I'll reup for a few more years. They are trying to convince me to. I am fifty-two, and the retirement age is between fifty-five and sixty. Not that far away.

He had wanted to take me to Phuket when we first met, but he got sick with a bout of malaria, and that trip never happened.

I am going with the flow, he says, his hand sweeping the air in front of his face. I remember that gesture. I wonder if I am part of the flow If that dinner—depending on its outcome—will help him make a final decision.

I love being in New York, he says. I haven't been back in seven years.

So, not since his last visit when we fought about the book I had written about David. My writing was always the specter that stood between me and men. Except David. At least, until he claimed that I had *ruined* his life with *that* book.

The food was delicious. He ate his, then polished off mine. Like he used to do. And the bottle, too, like I had predicted—you order a bottle, you'll drink three quarters and I'll drink the rest. How about you a third and me two-thirds? But I had been right. He talked about his daughter, I talked about mine, Juliet was married, with a baby. We raised our glasses to that. We carefully avoided all talk of recent romantic entanglements. Things were going well. We remembered the way we made coffee together at his place, and the very strong tea he always forgot at the bottom of the teapot that turned moldy. I recalled the first date we had in Paris, at La Coupole. The oysters. The Sancerre. The past was breezing back toward us.

It was time to bring it up. He had refilled my glass. I was still working on the first quarter of the bottle. I drank a little and glanced at him.

You know, hmmm… when you stopped responding to my calls and emails. It was cruel. You disappeared. You ghosted me.

Yes, I did. It was so burning inside of me, these horrible feelings of anger. He put his hand on his chest. It felt so bad. Such a horrible feeling. I just wanted to disappear.

Because of my book?

Yes.

Everything had been said back then. How he had begged me not to publish it. How he had offered me to come live with him in Geneva and he would support me and Louise while I wrote another book instead. Perhaps write a novel with him. He had literary aspirations. We were sitting on his bed, and I had felt all the blood rush to my face. No, I said, I can't do that. I am a writer. That's what I do. That's how I make my living. This book is not about you. Has nothing to do with you. I need to publish it. I knew it was the end then, but I couldn't bring myself to give it the final blow. And he couldn't bring himself to do it either. He cut all communications a few months later.

It was when you went to Kenya.

Yes.

It took me a long time to realize what was going on. I even called you when my uncle died because I wanted to share that with you. You had met him.

My feelings were too strong. I didn't want to have a nasty fight with you.

No need for a fight. You could have told me it was over. Even just in an email. Instead of me waiting without knowing. I am not attacking you. It's a long time ago now. It was really hard that there was no closure.

I know. I wanted to put everything behind me. When I came back from Kenya, I asked to be transferred to Lebanon. I didn't want to have anything left of that time.

We both stayed silent. I measured the betrayal he must have felt. He was open to me, vulnerable, at this moment. To even admit to the pain, that anger. The way he dealt with it by cutting all ties. Perhaps, for that reason, he had kept his image of me intact in his heart. We fall in love with an image. The hardest part, after a breakup, is to let go of the image.

I went back to Russia, I said. To Saint-Petersburg. For a literary seminar. The following year. My hotel was in the center. Kazanskaya Ulitsa. I could walk to the Hermitage, to the Neve. I could see the barges cruising at night when the drawbridges open up on the Neve River. Beautiful city.

Let me guess, it was during the White Nights?

Of course! The end of June.

I had looked for him there, for his ghost. The sound of Russian, the smoky clubs, Swan Lake at the Mariinsky Theater, echoing the Sleeping Beauty we had seen together on a New Year's Eve at the Bolshoï in Moscow. The iridescent waters of the Neva, the pastel of the palaces along the canals.

We were at dessert. I had ordered an *île flottante* for him, a meringue floating on a sumptuous sea of yellow custard; a *crème brûlée* for me—old fashioned, almost retro French desserts. He dipped his spoon in the *île flottante* and handed it to me. It tasted just like the one my grandmother made, the custard silky, the meringue softly crunching.

Remember the coffee we used to make in the little Italian moka pot with coffee you brought back from Paris? What did you call it?

What?

The espresso coffeemaker.

Oh! The Bialetti.

Right.

He was talking to me from a great divide. From another time I had left behind on the other side of the Atlantic, on the other side of my life. He was barely there, his body shimmering like a mirage. I felt barely there myself. An alter ego had those memories, had known that man.

An image of Jonah flashed across my mind. Jonah in the park, sitting on the bench, tuning his guitar, his hair falling over his forehead. His long, nimble fingers. How focused he was. How huddled unto himself, how most everything we shared in real life had been non-verbal despite the hundreds of texts we had exchanged.

I pushed the *crême brûlée*, almost untouched, toward Vadik.

You can have the rest, I said. I'm not hungry anymore.

He only had a taste, put the spoon down and placed his hand on mine across the table.

I remembered his hand, short, squarish fingers, soft skin. The hands of a man who doesn't use them for a living.

I remember how your hand felt, I said.

It was true. The memory of its texture.

I remember how yours felt, he said. The same as now.

I still thought it was a gesture of tenderness and abandoned my hand to his—or kind of abandoned it. My hand felt devoid of nerve endings, as if severed from the rest of my body. He turned it around and caressed the inside of it. It was not just tenderness. His touch became more insistent. And still I left my hand there, a fish stranded on the wet sand, waiting for the next wave to come and carry it back to sea. It was familiar, that touch. We had been lovers for almost six years. The intimacy lingered between us, a faint scent. We had shared days and nights and trips all over Europe, and sea vacation and ski trips, and champagne in hotel rooms, and passionate afternoons. The feeling of our hands together was a memory of that time, which I told myself had turned into tenderness.

My hand waited to be released.

The espresso was placed in front of him, a sliver of lemon on the saucer.

There's one thing you can't do in New York—smoke a cigarette while you drink your coffee.

As he picked up the cup with his right hand, his shirt slipped up, revealing his white, hairless arm. He had very little hair on his chest either. One of his grandfathers was a Buryat, he had told me. The Buryats were descendants of the Mongol tribes who lived on the central Asian steppes. Maybe that was the reason for his very straight hair. But he didn't like to think he had Asian blood. With a wave of desire, I thought of Jonah's arm, dark and hairy, and his chest with coils of dark, curly hair. His strong hands, his nervous fingers, a little rough from playing the guitar.

I pulled my hand out and wrapped it around my glass of wine.

How's the espresso?

Not that good.

I can tell from the smell. The best coffee in town is near my apartment, in a little café on 9th Street.

We should try it, he said.

I had a fleeting image of the two of us getting a cappuccino at the little café in the morning if he stayed the night. It was the café where I had gone with Jonah when we first met. Vadik didn't belong there.

He paid and took out a pack of Marlboro Reds, labeled with the usual sinister threat of death. In Cyrillic letters, it looked even more foreboding.

I have your bottle of vodka. He patted the bulging knapsack at his feet. And I bought a papaya at a fruit stand on Fourteenth Street on the way.

The papaya! He would split one in half, and we would eat it for breakfast in Geneva. How he liked to peel a fresh papaya in the morning. You could find them ripe just so at the nearby hypermarket, packaged in sealed, hard plastic so they wouldn't go bad. The long slices he carved, and then sucked on the flat kernel. They were exceptionally non-fiberish. Almost as good as in Thailand, he used to say.

The papaya and the vodka. He had come prepared.

It was a chilly May evening, too chilly for New York in May. And I was only wearing a jean jacket, which I buttoned up to my neck. He lit another cigarette outside the restaurant and wrapped his arm around me while we waited for a cab. I'll keep you warm, he said.

It was really chilly. It was nice to have the arm of a man around my waist. The Yellow Cabs flowed down Sixth Avenue in tight clumps. None of them were lit up.

Getting warmer?

Yes.

Me too.

I pulled away slightly.

Where do you take your train? I asked. What train station?

I knew he was staying at his friend's in Connecticut.

Grand Central. But I'm taking you home.

We were waiting at the corner of Sixth Avenue and 13th street and no cab in sight. I was shivering in my denim jacket, and he pressed me closer to him.

I am starting to have thoughts, he said.

I didn't want to lead him on. The longer we'd wait, the more he'd pressed me against him, and I'd have to confront him. I booked a Uber and we slipped into the seat. We cut across town on East 10th Street and drove along the park.

Remember the neighborhood?

Yes, of course. Why don't we go to the little café you mentioned?

It's just a café. It probably closes at eight or nine. I'm sure it's closed now.

The car made the right turn on my street.

Halfway down the block, I told the driver. Right hand side. By the fire hydrant.

Will you invite me up?

He was sitting really close to me. I wasn't sure whether his arm was around me. It was all a blur, but he was right there against me, and I felt confined—the vodka, the papaya and coffee for breakfast, the intense circle of the couple, it was too much. The ambiguity had dissolved. He was coming back, and it was over for me. He was bold, and I liked that. It would have been beautiful, a reunion seven years later, the triumph of love over adversity and misunderstanding. It would have been the kind of story of which romcoms are made, the happy ending, and I believed in love, in never ending desire, but was each ending supposed to be either Anna Karenina under the wheels of a train, or get into the fold and suffocate?

Our fate had been suspended for seven years—a full life cycle—what had not been said then was being said now. I had tried being a certain kind of woman with him. But I wasn't that woman anymore. Maybe I had never been. I couldn't put my feet back in the steps we had walked together.

I pulled away from his embrace and turned toward him.

No.

It was terribly abrupt. A definite no, clear and unambiguous. I should have eased him into it. Not offer my hand, not let him hold it, not let myself be warmed up in the street. Not talked about the little café down the street like some kind of invitation, a tease. I hadn't wanted to lead him on. I was testing myself, perhaps there was buried desire deep inside of me that could be reignited? He had lost some of his sexiness, his mystery. But it wasn't him. It was me. I was sure of it now. I had changed irremediably.

You're taking me by surprise, I said. So much has happened since last we saw each other.

Yes, it's true.

The car pulled up in front of her building.

Will you keep the car?

He leant into my ear and whispered: not if you invite me up.

He was playing his last card. What had happened? Had he wanted that from the very first phone call he had made? Had he been encouraged because I had asked our mutual friends about him a few months ago? Had he assumed we would be on the same page?

No, I said. I just want to go home.

I don't remember what he said, maybe nothing, or even if I kissed him goodbye. I didn't give him any time to react. I opened the door and slipped out of the car and firmly closed it behind me. Breathed the cool air with relief. A taste of freedom and possibilities.

I didn't meet my father until I was in my forties, and after a long, torturous lunch in a little Provençal village in the south of France, he had walked me to my car. I had had a similar sense of escaping, of freedom, as I gunned the gas and waved to him from my open window.

When I got back upstairs, I realized that Vadik had forgotten to give me the bottle of vodka. Maybe he hadn't forgotten. It wasn't an oversight. The bottle of vodka was meant for both of us, we would have opened it together, and the papaya he had bought on the way would have been for our breakfast.

68

WANNA GO TO a film party with me?

A text from Lena. Tonight. Might be fun. UWS. Great place. Terrace overlooking the Hudson. Interesting people.

During the summer in Paris, I had bought a pretty top from a cool French designer. Draped tight around the waist and hips. Fresh and sexy, but in black and white plaid cotton, which made it look casual and not trying too hard. It would be a perfect opportunity to debut it. Change my mood. Be frivolous. Vadik's reappearance had confused me. But even more so, my reaction to his advances. *Brava*! a friend had complimented me when I told her I had turned him down. Why *brava*? It didn't cost me anything. I had no desire to be with him. Were you not tempted, even a little bit? my friend insisted. She thought I had acted out of feminist righteousness. Nope. None. If I had wanted him, I would have gone with him. I didn't stand on principle.

I hadn't heard from Jonah since I had gone to his place. Even though I had decided to stop contacting him, the craving was still there. When I zipped up my new top and buckled my sandals, I felt my spine straighten. I liked the image the mirror reflected. Turning down Vadik had been beneficial for my mental state. I took a selfie, then deleted it. Enough.

The party was in a triplex belonging to a well-known movie producer. A large open space buzzing, lavish food on all surfaces, a terrace crowded with smokers. Major art works on the wall. Even a small Picasso demurely hanging between two windows. Lena knew a lot of people and introduced me as we went around the room, clutching our flutes of champagne. But after thirty minutes, I had an urge to disappear in the ladies room and escape. It's hard handling these big New York parties unless you're part of that particular scene or that particular industry, or you've had a recent success. Just then, Lena pulled on my arm.

Judd Burnstein's here.

I recognized him right away. From his interviews, photos of him at awards shows. He was one of the hottest directors of his generation. Late forties. He had already signed a dozen films—two of them had been shown at Cannes. He had built his own little empire producing films and TV series. His wife, an actress, was starting to direct too.

He was standing by the door to the terrace, surrounded by people. I stared at him, trying to see the resemblance with Jonah. There was a likeness, but like a less successful collage of the same genes. Where Jonah was strikingly handsome in a brooding, dark kind of way, Judd was more plain, similar fine features but unremarkable. A little shorter than Jonah, he had thick framed glasses and graying hair escaping from a LA Dodgers cap.

Do you want to meet him?

Lena seemed excited at the prospect of this little bit of theater, of action. Vicariously. Or maybe she was thinking in terms of directing, how she would set the scene, how I would play it. How the brother would play it.

He's very cool, she insisted. I was at a panel with him a few weeks ago, and I invited him to give a master class next semester. I'll introduce you.

We waited for the circle to loosen around him, and Lena went straight to him, hugged him, and introduced me as Eve, my friend, a wonderful writer.

Screenwriter?

Not really. Only occasionally, I said. Novelist, rather. Big fan of your work.

Thanks.

He looked open and not at all pretentious. We moved to the drinks table, and he ordered champagne from the server.

Lena caught up with him from the last time they saw each other. Then he asked me if he might have heard of one of my novels. And when I mentioned the one about my divorce, he said he'd read it, had loved it.

Really? I was flattered. Nothing like someone mentioning they like your work to help you warm up to them.

And then suddenly, maybe because I had been flattered, maybe because I was starting to feel the second glass of champagne, I heard myself blurt out, as though a spring had sprung, I know your brother.

You do? You know Jonah? Are you a musician as well?

No, no. I just like the kind of music he plays. I go to a lot of jazz… experimental music concerts.

Did I imagine he looked at me differently? His eyes were on me, turning cooler as one does when an unexpected, maybe unpleasant topic of conversation has been brought up. Maybe I was projecting. Or he was just surprised.

I just saw him yesterday, he said. We don't get together that often. I'm in LA, and he's touring all the time. Do you know him well?

Had his tone changed? I hesitated for an instant. Tried to settle my voice on neutral.

I know him very slightly.

He looked at me intensely, searching, trying to assess my relationship to his brother. Was I just a fan? A friend? More? He had to be aware of the age difference. Nah. It probably wouldn't even cross his mind.

He scored my first two films.

He's very good, said Lena. The music he wrote for *Baby Girl* is great.

Yeah. Well. He doesn't like Hollywood. He could do very well. But… He's a purist.

I think he likes to play maybe more than to compose, I said. He seems to be very much sought after as a sideman.

I felt like an impostor talking about Jonah as if we had truly been involved. But I couldn't help myself. Just as I had shown his picture to my friends from Paris, I wanted to talk about him, make my bond with him alive to others, publicly, and even more to myself. What impression would his brother get? Would he tell Jonah he'd met this French woman who knew him? Would Jonah immediately guess it was me and feel exposed, betrayed?

It's a hard life. He could have a fantastic career in film. I wish he'd settle down. But he's always been mercurial. Carefree.

Except with that German girl, he almost got married… But she broke it up. She went back to Berlin. He took it hard.

The German girl. Almost married. Didn't he know they were actually married? Jonah really played his cards close to the vest.

Judd was talking like the father of a difficult teenager. I was surprised. Not surprised that he said that, because it explained why Jonah was so concerned his brother would find out about us. But surprised that he would tell me, a complete stranger. But perhaps, because I was older, he thought he could confide in me.

A young woman leaned toward him and whispered in his ear.

Sure, sure, he said. He turned to me. Excuse me, gotta go. Nice meeting ya! And Lena, we have to talk, I have a project I think you might be interested in… A TV series…

Lena and I barely had a chance to exchange a look than a young man, who may have been intrigued seeing us speak with Judd Burnstein, came up to us.

Cool look, he said. I noticed you from a distance. Are you French?

Is it that obvious? Yeah, actually. I am.

I worked with Judd on his last shoot in Paris. You reminded me of older women who live there. I hope you don't mind my saying that.

No. Not at all. *Au contraire!*

I felt grateful for his comment, especially as he seemed to be saying it spontaneously, without ulterior motive.

He was an assistant DP, mainly working on TV shows shooting in the city until he got hired in another film production. He was cute in a generic way, beard and sneakers, not unlike Jonah, but more self-assured.

We chatted for a while, and then I looked for Lena who had left us alone. I was eager to leave. I wondered if there would be repercussions to my mentioning Jonah to his brother. If they met again while Judd was in New York, the encounter would still be fresh in his mind and he might tell Jonah, but if they didn't get together right away, by the time the brothers would meet up again, that conversation would have been long forgotten.

69

IN OCTOBER, I attended a conference given by a well-known artist who had been active politically during the Vietnam War. He was presenting a series of paintings he had done after the release of his FBI files, using the real FBI files, with names redacted, and over which he had painted his signature abstract brushstrokes. Kirsty and Mark were friends with him and had invited me along. The show was in an art gallery in Bushwick. The room was full, everybody sitting on folding chairs. In the middle of the talk, a message popped on my phone. It was from my half-brother.

Notre père est mort hier d'une chute. Il avait 92 ans.

Our father passed away yesterday from a fall. He was ninety-two. "*Our*" father. *Notre père. Our father who art in heaven*... I recoiled at the use of the words "our" and "father." That man had never been "my" father. At the same time, as if by reflex, my eyes filled up at the words "father" and "passed away." I told my friends the news. They commiserated as though he had really been my father and I was grieving. I got up and left the room. My half-brother added that he was going to be buried the next day after a mass in the afternoon. It would be the morning for me. I wrote I would join them in spirit. The whole building hosted art galleries and artists' studios. I wandered around and peeked into the other galleries without paying any attention. I wanted to feel the mechanical movement of my legs, the regular intake and outtake of my breathing. I couldn't conjure any pain in my stomach, in my chest, in my throat. I hardly knew that man. And yet my whole body felt leaden.

Kirsty and Mark met me at a café after the conference, near the Morgan Avenue subway stop, which happened to be just a block away from Louise's apartment.

They expressed their condolences. I felt physically shook up but not in pain. He hadn't even been ill. He'd been sitting on a low wall above a street, and he lost his balance. His head struck the cobblestones. The scene played in my mind in detail. I imagined a little street tucked away in a labyrinth of narrow alleyways in the 10th or the 18th, and him sitting there taking a break from a tiring walk, a street winding down below. And then stumbling, falling. Hitting his head on the pavement. A good death, no illness. No decline.

It's strange. I don't feel anything. Just emptiness.

I tried to explain that I hardly knew him.

He had been reluctant, at first, to meet me. I had sent him a letter. My mother still had his old address from thirty years back in Nice, and he hadn't moved, apparently. And then I didn't hear back. Every day I checked the mailbox in the hope of seeing a French stamp, heart beating, as though I was waiting to hear from a lover. Finally, three weeks or so later a letter came, very formal, addressing me as *Madame*. I read it in my car, alone, weeping with relief that he had finally recognized my existence. The next summer I met him in a little Provençal restaurant half-way between Nice, where he lived, and the perched village where my mother had a house. I was forty-seven. Later I went to see him in Nice with Louise, who was seven and had insisted on meeting her "grandfather," and another time in Paris, where he introduced me to his sons and their families as his "daughter from New York." His daughter had refused to meet me. We exchanged Christmas cards for a few years after that, and then our correspondence eventually stopped. But he had introduced me to his family. I had gotten him to acknowledge my existence, which, in retrospect, may have been the whole point.

When my mother died a few years later, I invited him to the funeral—and he came. Perhaps, like the child of separated parents, even if they had separated before I was born and had never really been together, I had secretly wished for a reunion, even a posthumous one.

My half-brother texted a picture of my father taken around the time I was born. I showed it to Kirsty and Mark. Pale eyes. Lips slightly open. The face of a sensitive boy, with a hint of feminine softness. Dark jacket. White shirt, club tie, pocket square. The only hint of rebellion was the lit cigarette he held between his middle and fourth fingers. Maybe it was a touch of dandyism. I remembered the picture I had been shown as a child, blond, wavy hair combed back, argyle sweater, shirt collar open on the V neck. Casual cool of the time.

I searched for a headshot of my mother on my phone. Glamorous looks, hair tumbling in loose waves to one side, full lips, white collar with a discreet ruffle open on her throat. In a line-up of movie stars, from Marilyn Monroe to Sophia Loren, she wouldn't have been out of place. I showed both pictures to my friends.

Wow, they said. Cool couple.

They were right. At least for the time it took for their romance to flourish and die—the med school student from a good provincial family sowing his wild oats in Paris with the bad girl, ten years older, sexy, sophisticated Parisian, reckless. But they were never a couple. It was an accidental encounter.

You look like her, they said.

70

WHEN I GOT home from Brooklyn, I was numb, waiting for emotions to appear, to possess me, to invade me so that I wouldn't carry the burden of being myself, waiting for a catharsis, but I was cold sober.

I texted Jonah. Like throwing a sort of lifeline. Not expecting any response. I hadn't seen him since April when I had gone to his place. He had texted me several times, and I had never answered. There was nothing to explain.

Two minutes later he came on.

Hey! What's up? As if we could always pick up where we had left off.

Can I see you?

When?

Now.

I am rehearsing. Big concert tomorrow. I really have to stay home.

No, of course. That's okay.

Silence. And then the little dots got busy.

I mean… Unless… you want to come over.

How many times had I driven across the Williamsburg Bridge after the split with David. On Saturday nights, when Louise was at her dad's, the Williamsburg was my freedom bridge, the cars in a jam, chomping at the bit, headlights to headlights, the promise of another, lighter outcome to fill out the void in my own life, and the coming back at dawn, a flash of pink in the rearview mirror, peaking over Brooklyn, exhausted from a night gloriously spent. There was hardly any traffic tonight on the bridge. I was at his door in less than fifteen minutes. He hurtled down the stairs in his flip-flops to let me in. I removed sneakers, jacket in the kitchen, stood in my jeans and socks by his keyboard. I hadn't even thought of changing. His desktop computer was turned on, displaying a sheet of music, one of his guitar lying on its side.

You okay?

I don't know. Hold me.

What? What's going on?

He took me to the couch and sat with me, his arm around me.

Talk to me. What happened?

My father passed away.

I felt my eyes fill with tears again as though I was truly mourning a beloved father.

What? I'm so sorry.

I buried my head in his lap. I could feel him. It was reassuring, his desire for me.

No. It's not what you think. I barely knew him. Only met him a couple of times. I just found out today.

He placed his hand on my head and gently, tentatively, stroked my hair, as though I was a rescued animal and he wanted to send reassuring vibes, but he wasn't sure how to handle me.

I don't know why I'm reacting this way. He was nobody. I barely knew him. Do you understand?

Yes.

I thought of the newspaper clipping taped to his fridge of his father sitting in his office with the plaque in Hebrew. So impersonal. And yet he wanted to have it there, displayed next to him, and his father had given him the orchids—the ones that lived just on air. Even the most tenuous relationships can touch you deep, precisely because they are so tenuous. Because they make you feel that there could be something else. I dried my eyes with the back of my hand and sat up.

I'm sorry. I shouldn't have come.

It's okay. You want something to drink?

Okay.

Water? I have some beer.

Do you have Heineken?

He laughed.

Nope!

We shared the bottle, passed it back and forth. I leaned against him, and he kissed me on the lips and ran his hand down my breasts, inside my shirt, gently unzipped my jeans and pulled them down, pressed his hand between my legs.

Come, he said, and he took me to his bed.

There were no tights to rip, there was no mirror facing the couch, just a clip-on light on a shelf over the keyboard, right against the head of the bed. It was dark except for a Blue Moon sign across the street pulsing a beam of blue against the wall.

He was gentle, no acrobatics, no orchestrated moves. Afterward he held me against his chest.

I'm glad you came, he said.

Me too.

You're awesome. I just wish…

I laughed teasingly. That I was younger?

That we were closer in age.

We stayed a moment like this, without speaking. I felt at peace. And then he pulled away from me and sat up.

You're going to hate me, he said. I have to work.

Okay. But do you mind if I stay a little? You can work. I'll be quiet. You won't have to pay attention to me. I'll call a car in a bit. Would that be weird?

He hesitated.

Are you sure? It's going to be boring.

I won't stay long. I just want to listen to you.

I got dressed and lay down on the couch on my side, my legs folded, watching him. He ruffled through his music sheets, sat down, and picked up his guitar.

This was what I yearned for, that creative intimacy, that I had shared with David so many years ago, when we were both writing, each in our study, an invisible cloud enveloping us. I craved it perhaps even more than sex. I couldn't tell whether Jonah was pleased to have an audience or if he had only accepted because he wanted to offer me some solace and he felt compassion. He looked like he could shut down and pretend I wasn't there. I let the music—abrupt, syncopated, repetitive, angular, rough, with surprising bits of melody—penetrate me. I wanted to be in his aura.

I knew the moment wouldn't last, that I would have to leave soon, that it was stolen intimacy, stolen time. I intently took it all in, the fireplace with the books on the mantle, the unmade bed with the comforter we had tossed aside to have sex, the books on the shelf behind it, and in the dark, at the other end of the apartment, the door cracked open to the tiny bathroom, the orchids profiled against the kitchen windows, a pale moonlight shining through, the nine guitars hanging on the wall in their black cases. Jonah's body crouched over his tenth guitar, his knee rhythmically going up and down, his back hunched over.

I tried to remember all the details in case it never happened again. I thought I had gone too far asking to stay. I was imposing. And yet he had agreed. The neon sign was washing the living room with blue light. There was a pool of light from the clip-on lamp attached to a shelf above the keyboard. It threw shadows all around him, jagged and menacing when he moved. We were deep into East Williamsburg, and it was eerily silent. The whole situation was surreal, a stage for a play. He played the talented guitarist, and I played the grieving writer who observed the scene, who took mental notes. He was already gone, lost in his music, focused on the technical difficulties. I could tell by the way he played and replayed certain passages. He was becoming oblivious to my presence. I was lost in my cone of darkness and silence. He was receding farther and farther away. I picked up my phone and booked a ride back to Manhattan. The app said the driver would be there in seven minutes. I tiptoed past him. I silently put my sneakers back on, my jacket, my scarf.

He looked up for a second.

You're leaving?

Yes.

He got up and took me in his arms and held me.

Shall I walk you downstairs?

No. I'm good.

He kissed me again at the door. A long and almost romantic kiss.

Downstairs I sat on the stoop waiting for the car. It was chilly. The afternoon in the art gallery in Bushwick was only a few hours ago, but it seemed to have happened in another lifetime, to someone else. I held my knees tight. The street was deserted. The Blue Moon neon sign over my head was blinking. I watched out for the headlights of the car, but it wasn't coming. I felt light as air, as if a door had closed and on the other side of the door was a black void. Who was I grieving? My father that I barely knew? David, whom I had clung to desperately as a substitute father way longer than I should have after he confessed he had fallen in love with a woman who was in every way better than I was, a San Francisco flower girl turned superstar tech engineer, harder-working than me, braver, younger, bolder, tougher, a true warrior? He didn't say that. Not exactly in those terms. What he said was: She's a working girl, meaning (I thought) not like you who's staying home to write. Not like you, pretentious bourgeois-bohemian Eurotrash. I was grateful Jonah had given me shelter, had let me share his intimacy. Had comforted me. I thought of Vadik, who had tried to love me in the only way he knew.

The car almost missed me, passed the building, hit the brakes in a screeching of tires, and backtracked. I gathered my bag and got in. Off the Williamsburg Bridge, the driver made the familiar right turn on Clinton Street, and I felt a sense of relief, getting back to my territory, the place I had made my home.

71

I KNEW GOING back to him had been a mistake. Despite my better judgment, I started hoping again. Every week, the days when he came to work at the studio, I waited for a text, even just a "hey" casually tossed my way. Week after week I longed to hear from him. And then one day, two months later in mid-December, I ran into him while I was on my way to buy groceries. I had timed myself to go out when he usually left work, hoping our paths would cross. I saw him walking down the avenue carrying two heavy bags of equipment. A flash of desire tore at my heart.

He was parked a block away from my place. We walked side by side toward his car.

I'm in a hurry, he said, raising his bags as evidence. I need to deliver this.

I didn't say anything. I could feel the pull between us.

How are you?

Good, I said, keeping my voice breezy. I finished my screenplay. I just signed the contract. The film is going to be produced in France. We're shooting in April.

Wow! Congratulations. That's fantastic!

Thanks.

I'm sorry, he said.

Sorry for what? I could hear the edge in my voice.

He shook his head. His eyes met mine for a fraction of a second, but he didn't say anything. He didn't say a word about my father, about that time when he had held me in his arms in his apartment and he had comforted me and he had said things to me he probably regretted or had forgotten about.

He put his bags down and inserted the key into the lock of the door.

We were standing face-to-face. My heart was pounding. He hesitated.

I should really go. I have a rehearsal in Park Slope. I'm sorry. I wish things were different.

His voice was cold, now. Distant. He opened the door, tossed his bags on the backseat, and stood back up with his key his hand.

Well, goodbye then, I said.

It was over for good now. At least, the brother never said a word. Our affair had fallen of its own weight like a ripe fruit in the grass, to be pecked at by birds with their hard little beaks. It couldn't be put back on the branch. I pictured it as a ripe fig, its purple velvet bursting, revealing the soft, red inner flesh. I would like to have picked it up and devoured it. I forgot about my groceries. I drifted around the neighborhood. I wanted to stay outside in the darkening New York City dusk, the juicy fig dripping down my chin. I walked across the park, sat on the bench where we had sat that time.

I knew he had gone as far as he could with me, perhaps even farther than he ever thought he could go. I remembered that time I had gotten pregnant by David, and I didn't feel I could go through it, because I was trying to finish a novel. And at that moment, that novel was the most important thing in the world for me. I was afraid I couldn't handle another child, that it wasn't right. I chose my writing. That, too, David never forgave me. But that's another story.

72

IN THE LODGE where the faculty and students were staying at the Boulder residency, all the occult, astrology, magic, and mindfulness sites had been blocked by the hotel. For fear, perhaps, of seeing the place turned into a den of iniquity. Witches stirring their cauldron or riding broomsticks in the wee hours, while the only ones out in the woods at night were students hanging from the trees, high on 'shrooms. But none of that stopped the group of writers from laying out tarot cards on New Year's Eve and trying to divine the future.

Someone turned on a playlist, and the song "You put a spell on me" came on. We were all sitting on the big leather chairs around the fireplace. While I waited for my turn to have my cards read, I realized I loved spells. I didn't aspire at all to a life without desire. Wouldn't life be dreary without us putting a spell on each other? A dry spell is a bout of life without spells, a long haul in the desert. A life without magic. We love our spells. They are the spice of life.

Someone got the death card. The death card isn't to be taken literally but as a metaphor for transformation. The death of what doesn't serve anymore to make room for the new.

I didn't get the death card, that symbol of deep changes. I got the magician, his right hand pointing to the heavens and his left toward the earth. That, too, was a card of transformation, but of talents into gold. And of love. Each and every one of my cards were about creating—music, poetry and song, artistic delight. The only ambiguity in the spread was the two of cups in the past position. The two of cups is about a powerful romantic connection, explained the poet who read the cards. But because it appeared in the past position, it meant the romantic connection had ended.

Was this about our affair, swept by the ebbing tide? Or was it about some other past romance—with Vadik, for instance, which was definitely done?

A wood fire was roaring in the lodge, but outside the windows, the Rockies loomed like a menacing sentinel. The tarot cards were stacked up and reshuffled by the next person waiting for an oracle, and the question remained unanswered.

When we went back to our rooms, it was the stroke of midnight back East, and for the first time in two years, I didn't send him a Happy New Year text.

I slept badly, waking up several times as though I had missed or forgotten something, or perhaps waiting for a sign from him or from the universe. It was hot, the dry heat pumping against the cold mountain air. I dreamt, but the next morning I had forgotten the dreams. I felt lighter. I had finally swept away his ghost.

I took my notebook out on the flight back from Denver. I picked up my story where I had left off, after I'd quit the writing group. I didn't write in a fever. The fever had abated. Jonah was not whipping me into a frenzy. Of desire, of craving his attention. I didn't know how I would finish the novella. But I was sure of one thing: I would not throw myself out the window. And now that Jonah had reignited my desire, my longing for love, maybe I would have it again in my life.

It was night when the cab back from the airport dropped me home. I felt the emptiness of my apartment as soon as I pushed the door open. But it wasn't empty-sad. It was spacious. Warm. Welcoming. I put my suitcase down and plugged in the Xmas tree lights. They glowed softly. It was so inviting, I wanted to dance, spread my arms wide. I looked at the open, uncluttered space. I was floating in it. David, whose presence had lingered in the apartment for years like the smell of an old joint you can never get rid of, David was gone. He was not creeping in the shadows, judging my moves, checking my moods. He didn't hover, suspended from the rafters, didn't sneak behind the Xmas tree, didn't whisper, over and over, that he was in love with someone else, that he had to follow his heart. His spirit had vanished.

So maybe I had it all wrong about the card. Maybe it wasn't about Jonah, whom I had been compelled to seduce, to win back, always afraid to lose. Maybe it wasn't even about Vadik. Maybe it was about David. Or maybe they were all one and the same.

The cat sitter had left some soup on the stove for me. I warmed it up, poured some in a bowl, and sat at the kitchen table. After ten days of hotel food, the soup was fragrant and nourishing. Kitty-the-cat jumped on my lap and burrowed under my elbow, her tiny pink tongue flashing under her moustache. In the dark I could see the windows of the next building, across from the garden, lit up, the big ailanthus tree shadowed against them. I had just received an email announcing that the developer next door hadn't gotten a permit to build from the city. At least for now, I still had my view of the garden, the trees, the ivy growing on the wall.

73

A FEW DAYS after coming back from Boulder, I saw that he was playing at an afternoon concert in the converted garage nearby where I often went to listen to experimental jazz.

The space closes with a rolling shutter covered with graffiti. There's no sign, just a narrow door that opens a few minutes before the concert. Cement floor and rows of folding chairs are angled toward the performance space. A basement where the musicians gather in-between sets. It isn't that cold for the beginning of January, but I am only wearing my black leather jacket and a woolen scarf wrapped around my neck, and I shiver. The composer, owner of the space, is there, the genius musician, so genius he has gotten a genius grant a few years back, so prolific he can't even keep up with the ferocity of his own output.

He's sitting at the little desk near the door, in cargo pants and a hoodie, taking the money. Hair cut short, round tortoise-shell glasses. He smiles at me. We're neighbors, I've seen him on the street before at the supermarket. We've chatted. It's okay, he says, waiving the price for me. Welcome! He gets up and gives me a hug. With his full lips, his glasses, his wide smile, his warmth, he makes me think of David, too. Ever since I met Jonah, David is everywhere. David, I've had to shut him down, nail him shut, after the divorce, and now he's hovering, but it's the David of the early days that I had fallen in love with, who's reincarnated in this band of musicians.

There's an energy to that scene, spreading in ever widening circles all the way to the far reaches of Brooklyn. The room is filling up. I've gotten in just in time. The dark room is bursting with people standing up against the sidewall several rows thick, filing to the back, where there are still available seats. No one is allowed to stand, by order of the fire department.

I remember this corner decades ago, a space right next to it. I dig into my memory, layers and layers of time, once-powdery sediments that have hardened and need to be drilled. What was it called? The Saint? No, World's End. A large, cavernous, raw space, where house music pulsed and ricocheted and shadows danced between black-washed walls. It was truly dangerous to venture that far east then. No cab ever accepted a ride that far, except I lived a few blocks north. A den of heroin, then crack, and up and down the avenue, the cries of *bajando, bajando*, echoing from one end of the block to the other, signaling that the man, the cop, the police car was slowly cruising, lights flashing, headlights sweeping over the used needles and little Ziploc bags stamped Poison, DOA or Overdose littering the gutters.

The genius composer moved to the neighborhood around the same time I did. We're almost the same age. Born the same day, even, a couple of years apart, according to his Wikipedia page. So uncanny. Twins of a kind. Kindred spirit. So, to open that space so close to that long-defunct club, was a continuation of sorts. Despite the rampant gentrification, the powerful vibes of the New York avant-garde are still here, the same spirit that attracted me three decades ago as a fatal fault line in which I stumbled when I met David.

Sold out, someone cries at the door, which is heavily curtained with thick black cloth. The musicians are arriving one by one. It's a quartet, two guitars, a bass, a percussionist. I don't see Jonah at first. And then he walks right by me. I am sitting in the third row, on the side. When he sees me, his face goes soft, and a big smile tinged with surprise lights up his eyes. His hair, curling almost to his shoulders. Dark beard and mustache. A little bent, I notice, as he walks to his spot, to the right, his guitar already there, waiting for him by the chair. White shirt with the sleeves rolled up, gray chinos, red high-top Converse. Because of the angle of the chairs, all I have to do is lean a bit to the side, and I have a perfect line of vision to him. His profile. His dark hair falling on his cheek that he keeps pushing back behind the ear.

The piece they are playing is intricate, atonal, syncopated. I am glad I have a good view of him because, with one guitar and a bass guitar in the band, the sounds blend, it can be hard to tell one from the other. I need to see his hands move, and his leaning over or leaning back, to better hear his sound.

The music tells a story, not a pretty, flowery melody, but the savage architecture of a drama. Even in these short, taut pieces, the drama captures me. The sudden soaring, the deafening banging, followed by the retreat; it's the movement that is thrilling, although there are fragments of melody, refrains, quotations, echoes of other, traditional music, klezmer's doleful melodies rushing into free jazz improv. But what stirs the soul, what excite the emotions, is the narrative arc, the dramatic ups and downs, the cliffhangers, the climb up to a climax, the coda.

He has his sheet music in front of him on a stand but takes flights of improvisation like a bird whose cage has suddenly been yanked open. I stare at his perfect profile, at the curve of his lips, at his hair curling in his neck—for fear that if my eyes wander, he might magically disappear. The intensity of his focus, of his posture, sitting motionless on the chair, while his hands fly, his fingers pick, sweep, tap. In the last piece, it's all about his guitar, with the backbeat of the bass behind him, the muted thump of the drum, slowly fading until he launches into a solo. I am stunned by the texture of sounds that arise from his hands. For a few minutes it is the rich, dirty tapestry of his sound that spin and spill over the room, gleefully luxuriating in its virtuosity, flying off into a divine moment, building to the climax. And then seamlessly the others rejoin, and it's the end of the piece, the end of the set. And the crowd clap, cheer.

He stands, a little shyly, a little awkwardly, bowing. He gives me a discreet wave, then disappears down the stairs, and when he shows up again, it's over already, that tiny moment; he's being called back to his friends, another musician he gets introduced to, who congratulates him. I wrap my scarf around my neck, zip my jacket, and walk out.

The wind is sharp on Avenue C, near Houston, I push my beanie down on my forehead. It's not the harsh New York winter of the past. No snowbank, not even any snow, but a sky of gray steel, gusts of wind, papers flying, neon illuminating the façade of the bodegas, even though it's only midafternoon. I take the overpass above the FDR Drive to go to the East River. I lean over the parapet, watching the tugboats chugging upriver, the Williamsburg Bridge in the distance. The wind is even sharper here, the smell of brine powerful, the seagulls sing their lonely cry. My chest swells with the brisk sea air, that sense of freedom that comes over me as soon as I get to the edge of the city.

At this moment, it doesn't matter if I never see him again. Because it's my world, too, my adopted world that he's helped me reconnect with. He is part of me now. Losing him is a small price to pay to have found myself again. A fog is descending upon the water. Brooklyn, on the other side, is already losing its contours. It's time to go home.

One day, before we broke up, I told David I didn't see myself growing old in this country. But it has become home now. I feel like I am putting roots deeper into my life.

About the Author

CATHERINE TEXIER is the author of six novels, including *Love Me Tender*, *Panic Blood*, *Victorine*, and *Russian Lessons*. Her memoir *Breakup* was an international bestseller. *Victorine* won *Elle Magazine's* "Readers' Best Novel of the Year" award in 2004. *Love Me Tender* was a *Village Voice* bestseller in 1987. Her work has been translated into ten languages, and has been widely reviewed in the national and international press. She has taught at Columbia University, University of Nebraska, Brooklyn College, Rutgers University and Hofstra University, and now teaches at the New School. She was born and raised in Paris, and lives in New York.

BOOKS BY ITNA

Urban Gothic: The Complete Stories
Bruce Benderson

Settlers Landing
Travis Jeppesen

Bruno's Conversion
Tsipi Keller

The Beads
David McConnell

The Virtuous Ones
Christopher Stoddard

Printed in the USA
CPSIA information can be obtained
at www.ICGtesting.com
JSHW032349180124
55540JS00006B/183

9 798988 282914